PO FOLK

I stand up for My Po Folk, 'Cause my Po Folk they know Folk
I'm talking 'bout somebody I can turn to when I need somewhere to go Folk.

I'm talking 'bout my sweet water, corn bread, home knitted bed spread–
Monetary Po Folk but filthy rich with love instead.

Them my people 'Cause they understand what it is to fight,
5 in the same bed staying warm through the coldest night.

My Po Folk just as humble,
They thank God for their blessing.
Know the value of a lesson,
Still praying for progression.

My Po Folk that'll probably see God fo' they see wealth,
Don't have a worry in the world as long as they in good health.

Me Tears

I'm talking 'bout getting down on they knees,
Cooking with gov'ment cheese,
Hand me down Goodwill coat in weather that's 20 degrees.

Them my people, we equal and I love all my Folk,
Richer or poorer but I lov'em most when we broke.
'Cause if we ever get rich then we tend to forget,
How we came up in this life when we ain't really have shit.

My Folk, not your Folk.
I'm talking 'bout my love ones in the struggle.
We needed money so we hustled,
 Times got hard, we flexed muscles.

My back yard Bar-B-Q-ing every first of the month checks.
My welfare recipients who fight to get out the projects.

My Po Folk my 'fa sho' Folk who

understand and know Folk.
God is my witness, I appreciate my
Po Folk

Gotta walk a mile to the bus stop, 2 jobs during the week Folk.
Party on the weekend knowing damn well that we broke Folk.

Them my people we equal through the struggle we push on.
My ghetto babies in school that can't wait to get their lunch on.

My pawn shop broke Folk who get paid on Friday,
and broke by Sad-day 'cause the rent went up highly.

Them My Folk my Po Folk my not a pot to piss in or a window to throw it out Folk.
If I ain't got it imma get, or learn how to do without, Folk.

My open up the oven to heat the house 'cause the heater broke Folk.
I'm talking about my go borrow a cup of

Me Tears

sugar and a pack kool-aid from next door Folk.

My put a hanger in the tv Folk, Holla' loud when you see Folk-folk.
Downtown shopping at the thrift shop freely Folk.

My "say bro can I hold a dime until I see you the next time?" Never get it back Folk.
Never in hell will I turn my back on my Po Folk.

My "Hey their young blood,
What's going on their cat daddy?"
My Old School Po Folk driving a broke down slant back caddy.

Them my people, I lov'em and I'll always be around,
For my people in the projects to my Folk that's locked down.

My check to check living Folk,
can't wait 'til Thanksgiving Folk.
My thank God it's Friday, now I can start

Me Tears

living Folk

Them my people we equal through the struggle we push on.
My ghetto babies in school that can't wait to get their lunch on.

My pawn shop broke Folk who get paid on Friday
and broke by Sad-day 'cause the rent went up highly.

Them My Folk, My Po Folk, My not a pot to piss in or a window to throw it out Folk.
If I ain't got it, imma get, or learn how to do without, Folk.

Them My Folk understand that I love all My Folk.
But My Po Folk, they keep it real with me 'cause we Folk and we know broke,
My Po Folk

By: Georgia Black-KILLEEN, TEXAS

Deapria Yvonne Shuler-McKnight My Baby Momma. Thank you so very much for all of the hard work you have put into our children, which helps us all get through. But mostly, I appreciate all you have done to allow me to reach for my dream of becoming the writer I aspire to be.

BABYGIRL

Coming Attractions

Awtuhm Duv
The Bird's Song
Book Three

The Ex-Wife, The Underdog
And The Comeback

Anthony G. Mcknight
'And The -G- Is For'

The AntiVote

Goons The End of Days

Mr. Biggs Women

BABYGIRL

By: Urb'n Anthony

URB'N ANTHONY

Copyright/Urb'n Anthony
All Rights Reserved

Publisher's Note:

This is a work of fiction. Names, characters, places, events, incidents, are not real. All references to actual people and or events are coincidental, and are products of the author's imagination. All resemblances to any persons living or dead, places and/or locals are entirely coincidental.

No part of this publication may be reproduced, stored transmitted or introduced into a retrieval system in any form. Or by any means electronic, mechanical, recording, photocopy, or otherwise without the written consent of the Author. This includes all literature by the author.

Awtuhm Duv: The Bird's Song

About The Author:

Author Urb'n Anthony was born in New Haven, Connecticut. He received his formal education at the University of New Haven in Marketing, Public Administration, and Education. Prefers a shot of Gin not beer, but if you buy will drink beer. Would love to go to Amsterdam and smoke until I cry. Don't like to call women bitches and whore, unless they don't know what they are................damn bitches.

Contact Urb'n:

Email: www.awtuhmduv@excite.com

Website: www.geocities.com/urbnanthony

On The Covers: Kelley Myers

Acknowledgments: God in All I Do.

    Without Water Today-
Without Food Tomorrow
        I Will Give Praise.

Copyright: All Rights Reserved

Awtuhm Duv: The Bird's Song

WRITE YOUR OWN REVIEW

Awtuhm Duv: The Bird's Song

Special Thanks to all of the African-American Bookstores for your support while I toured the country last year. Much respect to Jah-Flex for the Bob Marley CD, and Jah-Nice likewise. I would like to thank in particular Kelley Myers, Tara Fulton, and Sterling Daniels for the pictures they provided for the covers. Thanks to the brother Wil Baker for opening my book with such beautiful poetic art.

Okay, shouts out to all of the crew at the Rev. Dr. Martin Luther King Community Center in Milwaukee, Wisconsin.(Keanna, Jamon Smith, Breione, Breanna,Catrise, Nicolas, D'andre, Shana—hey Keanna keep singing. If you get through High School I may take you to the prom or something, just promise not to sing(smile). The Staff at the center—Keep up the good work. Much love to the all the peoples that past me the burgers, fries, pizzas, tacos and all while I was on the road.

As always much respect and love for all of my babies and my baby momma for all of the support and understanding. I don't want to be famous, or rich, I just love doing what I like to do, and that's trying

Awtuhm Duv: The Bird's Song

my best to make you all proud to call me daddy. Just remember, daddy can never be famous, only almost famous. That famous shit is for people who seek others approval. I always stand alone. It's up to you all to stand by me-together, and likewise--------I Love You, TheGreatDaddini.

Awtuhm Duv: The Bird's Song

Introduction

    Although many talk about the street life, and being a gangsta, not many know the history of it all and why they do what they do. They can't give account as to why they die. Even more telling is the fact that many, especially today will use the phrase 'Gansta Rap', knowing all of those that began the phenomenon in past years. They pay respect to the founders. That's admirable, but in our line of doing, we don't boast. It's a quiet and calm thing. A fool brags about criminal shit.

    'Being about it' was once more important than 'talking about it'. When people started to talk about 'the life', it made space for the informers, rumors and myth. When it all started for the inner city youth, the blacks especially, It was difficult to tell one from the other. It was impossible to detect honor, as it was all built from lies, dishonor and bloodshed.

    History is key to knowing, and American Gansta for the Negro truly began outside of America. It started in and

Awtuhm Duv: The Bird's Song

around 1961. The world shaped this event, and it started over global politics.

Now, many will try to deny this point. But, so what, it's true. The Cuban Missel Crisis was the doom for the inner city youth here in this country. That one factor was like adding an even more potent fuel to the fires already burning in this country, if possible. Our leaders did nothing to make matters better. In fact, with so many things happening during this period, it made it impossible to focus in on our domestic situation, our neighbor-hoods, especially when it was said to be more troublesome international problems looming. The other factors of racism, and the Vietnam War which took place in that decade helped. So many things, and so much pain occurred during this time that people needed medication, they needed drugs.

The political unrest in the Carribean Islands took center stage, and that was all that was needed to begin the urban downfall we witness today in this country. The opening up of those islands became the gateway to the deterioration of this country. Don't get it twisted, not all islanders are bad. Not so much the people

Awtuhm Duv: The Bird's Song

as a whole, it was our policy.

However, you can't blame the Negro for this. It was White America who supported this occurrence. In fighting against communism, this country created a fear, and panic unprecedented in modern times. It wasn't the Redcoats this time. The Russians were coming, only through Cuba during the Cold War Era. they were going to plant nuclear weapons in our backyard.

This rhetoric blinded the people to what really became the issue. This scare created a climate where deals were being made with friends and foes alike. In the islands, this country used its influence in every Carribean country to gain a foot hold for Democracy rather than Socialistic, or Communistic political policy.

Along this line, it is easy to understand why they killed President Kennedy. "They" certainly weren't the communist government of Cuba. If that were the case, Castro would have been long done away with. The Castro Theory was just a smoke screen for some Americans. What would have been genius would have been the Mafia. However, that too is highly improbable. Just think. The most likely people to benefit from a Kennedy assassination would be the people with the most opportunity, and feared communism the most. That group would be the wealthy Texans and more so the Republicans. The simple fact that LBJ was a democrat mattered not. A Texan is a Texan. When all is said and done, and push comes to shove, there is only one politic------- Money.

The End

    Why is this shit going on like this? How in the hell did I step into some shit like this? Mafucka on his knees and shit. Worst of all my babies and mamma ain't what's on my mind. How did she know about shit like this? I should have listened to her. Those damn trees. I sort of understand them shits right about now. I only seen them once. It was on a drive through Louisiana when I noticed them. The same sadness I felt, wondering, as we drove through the Bayou catches me today. Only thing, it's me alone this time. Just as those Cypress trees appear to have their own sorrow, standing in the water by themselves, not pretty at all.

    This shit ain't pretty either. They have their sorrow, and I feel it too. Cypress sorrow is a muthafucka. I bet if you could command them to fall the fuck over they would. Just imagine standing in that cold water, when it's cold. I don't know if I want to make it from this shit, or hope someone squeezes the damn trigger. It's better than being in this position. Yeah,

Cypress sorrow is a bitch. Most of all, seeing a nigga dead next to you, and blood coming from his head ain't the best of situations. "Watch your company," my mother would say. I really don't want to be in his company now, not beside that dead nigga. The end isn't always the best place to start, but damn. This shit started years ago, and in a country not too far away. But fuck just telling about how other mafuckas died and shit. My pain, that's what I need. I want niggas to feel my pain. This is how my pain began. It started in Jamaica.

Jamaica

This country, more than any other in the island nations of the Carribean mirrored the images of colonialism. Castro and Communism didn't move in as was the fear in the 1960's, nor did the Mafia. It was the CIA. It was the American money that supplied the Jamaicans fighting for independence. It was this country that supplied weapons and alike to forces in that country to destabilize the socialist movement within the country of Jamaica. Through constant violence, and assassinations political parties were formed. America wanted and could deal with any form of government as long as it wasn't communism. Socialism was considered middle of the road, which meant it was closer to democracy and could be nudged a bit farther. It could be worked with. Not to mention Vietnam which distracted many people from seeing the damage about to take place in the Carribean.

It was in these negotiations and deals with locals within Jamaica that this country tore away another layer of its 'so-called' fiber. You see, not only were the Americans getting what they wanted(because in the inner cities of Jamaica, being black was everything), it was the "Black Face" which masked the deeds of America.

With the smuggling of weapons into the country, came the smuggling of marijuana out of the country. People were too stoned in those days to wonder how all of this weed was getting into the country. All of the hippies fighting against what America was doing in the world were getting high from a byproduct of this nations policy. That's right, Bob Dillon and

Awtuhm Duv: The Bird's Song

all of the peace sayers where fighting Vietnam, but on the other hand smoking some of the best smoke that the CIA could provide. Ignorance is truly bliss, and that's the best part about listening to the old time rock-n-rollers.

    This country funded the trade policies of the Jamaican Island, by allowing Mary Jane into our country. America became an undercover trade partner with people of whom they knew nothing about. This was to be a preview of future foreign policy and covert operations, such as the Cocaine smuggling and the future Noriega bullshit.

    Now, in this period of time, is how marijuana received such a bad rap. Just imagine, a weed from the ground being given a Class One rating by our government in the 2000 era. Marijuana is ranked along side PCP and other drugs as being useless and having no medicinal value. That's what the marijuana trade of the seventies did. First, this government thought it would qual the people. Then, it found out that the weed brought a different sort of mental state within the people.

    It was cheap, and non-addictive. Not only which, it was accessible and anyone could grow it, which meant it couldn't be

Awtuhm Duv: The Bird's Song

controlled. That's what our government wanted. They wanted to control the people. Now, that's the difference between weed and cocaine. Doctors can prescribe cocaine derivatives that are addictive but not weed which is not. Cocaine is rated as less harmful than Marijuana. It's rated so, because Americans can't produce cocaine, and as long as the source is foreign, it can be pinpointed. Just watch a base head. They will always go back to the source. For base, a crack head will snitch out his mamma. But weed, weed makes a nigga say: "Fuck You," then laugh at your ass.

All one has to do is watch that Woody character on that 'Cheers' show. In retrospect it isn't hard to understand what made the mafucka so mellow. We find out later through the media that he was a pot head. Everyone likes to be around the dude, but no one wants to admit they smoke. But, they love Woody because they know that mafucka has some good-ass smoke.

To this end, America became drug partners with other countries. America became an undercover trade partner with people of whom they knew nothing about.

This was to be a preview of future foreign policy and covert operations {Such as the cocaine scandals of the eighties and nineties}. Sure, the nation changed in the eighties, but America allowed the same courtesy to South American cocaine producing countries. However, in this look, we will focus on matters concerning street life involving the players from earlier days.

The Youth

From my age seven, the story was begun to be told to me by my mother in bits and pieces. Every opportunity she had, the story would be filled in, in parts. It was if I had to know this. It was like her channel was stuck, like the history channel on television that I tried to avoid at all cost. She would keep playing the same tune about how Dez was a wicked man, and gave reasons as to why I should stay away from him. I was warned to also stay away from his children. It's not that I didn't want to learn it. I just couldn't understand it.

The old arrogant woman down the street knew, as she looked at me certainly more weird, as time went by. She rocked in the porch chair for days, they called her Mamma Auntie, my mother didn't like her one bit. "Stay the fuck away from that crazy-ass bitch. You hear me?" She would tell me, because she said the woman did roots or something.

Now that I'm older, I can repeat and respect the story, although I don't understand it in full. That, could never be told. I was told more each time before things were added to the past of which I have no part of.

"Oh, the 1960's," mama would wail, as if it were the date or dates she despised and not the people. Like the people on the news hate the guns and not the people that use them. I had no idea what this all had to do with me. I didn't do anything. Rather than talk, the woman on the porch began to shake a stick which had a bell attached to it. I had no idea what that meant. But who cares?

Awtuhm Duv. The Bird's Song

Dez

    Some say that life on earth started with Adam. Well, the problems of our inner city as it relates to the drug trade started with Dezmond. It was he, picked by our government to lead an insurgence against the established government of Jamaica. Although he grew up in the slums of Kingston, he was smarter than most, and knew the value of his life was minimal, and decided to find his own way out, he wasn't interested in being loyal to this homeland. Instead, he decided to trade it in, to trade up.

    The skinny, tall, yet well spoken rebel in the city jungle had several ways in which he learned to survive. No matter the technique, he had to feed off of the people. They had to. People were the only resource found in the city. Because of the upheaval, there was no work, and power was in the hands of those that had a 'say' in the everyday life and death struggles. The power of the city was in the basic levels of those who held territory on the streets. Power was not through intellect, but in the understanding of who toted the most weapon firepower. This was made possible because of the poverty. The residents of Kingston and throughout the other cities were reliant upon scraps for survival, even from the city dump they survived.   It was fate then that brought Dez to the forefront.

    The CIA needed an operative, and Dez had a clan established that had the means to get stronger. Along with the weapons he was furnished, he also was given something even more precious. He was given a great weapon, the ability to feed the people, his people, those that supported him. In a hungry country, starving for the basic necessities of life, It isn't difficult to understand why he had a following if only physical. Many hated him, but he fed his supporters.

    As the years past it was more of interest for Dez to find out about things outside of the island, and he made several trips to the city of Miami. It was there, after being allowed to build a home and establish residence, that he decided to not only fight the struggle on his homeland. He became the businessman. The idea grabbed him like the snake he was. He made acquaintances with the people on the island and created a network by which to obtain marijuana from the growers.

Marijuana was by no means the drug of choice in America at the time. It was usually, and almost exclusively used by the mountain men, the Rasta. Dez was far from being Rasta. Instead he worked on common ground. They had the weed, and he had the money. It was now that he began to work both sides of the issue. On the one hand, by dealing in Marijuana he provided capital to the native people of Jamaica to carry on their campaigns against America. On the other hand, he became well off and blinded by his own greed. It was his greed and wanting to be more capitalistic, and not for the cause of freeing Jamaica which became his obsession. It didn't matter the transaction, for the people or for the governments, he wanted his share.

The fighting escalated on the island, as through the trade, rebel forces amassed better weapons. Not only which, the forces of good was being pinpointed to the mountains, and it is in this that Dez betrayal began his demise. In a meeting with his handlers, Dez stepped up his game a bit more. He dealt with Johnny, a house nigger or Yankee to the people. At least that's what Dez and his crew called him behind his back.

They, Dez and his crew, had no idea as to what a "House Nigger," or an "Uncle Sam" was. True to form, when it was explained to him, Dez let out the biggest bellow anyone could imagine. If you didn't know better, you may have thought he ate a big meal or something, looking at the expression from his face. "Yes, yes," he smiled. "I love this America idea already....yeah," nodding his head. Then, the meeting.

"How is it that the people continue to resist?" He was asked by his handlers. "The people have them own rhythm," Dez answered

"What do you mean?"
"The rhythm of the people is in them music. The music is what make them strong. It is a spiritual thing, not from the earth. It is a mystical force which make them people rebel. Weapons won't cure the movement."

"Who make the rhythm?"
"Them have music men."

"Who?"

"The Rasta.....The music is to them like water for the body."

"But you trade the weed that they grow, and it's you who give them the means to be strong against us."

"I know nothing about any means, or no weed," Dez was irritated.

"You handle this music, and Rasta business," he was told.

"Where me live then?"

"You act like an American, you live in America."

That's all Dez needed to hear. He didn't need Jamaica anymore. Besides he had roots there, and several loyal followers. He became the hand for this government within that country. However, he underestimated the earth force in the mountains.

  As reggae became more popular in the mid-1970's the United States became increasingly nervous. As the people of this country became enamored with the culture of Jamaica. Even white America began not only embracing the marijuana openly, white people in America began to follow Rastafari, and becoming dreads. That's why until this day the American government outlaws marijuana. They don't want their white babies humbling themselves to a black God. What was being won geographically on the island, was being lost in the hearts and minds of the people. Then, the most costly decision was made. They tried to silence the music, and the source.

Awtuhm Duv: The Bird's Song

Kingston

In the seventies it was Dez who lead a faction in the city of Kingston to rebel against the government for the people. He had all the help he needed and this is how he got richer than most. With all the arms, weapons and supplies he needed, he was greedy and seized yet another opportunity. He used his strength to travel back and forth from the island to the city of Miami.

Not one to waste time, and to maximize his efforts, Dezmond began to transport by the pounds at first then by the tons, huge amounts of the best smoke produced on the island. His efforts went unabated because not only was he an informer, he was a facilitator for the United States. This being said, he was given carte blanche, especially after 1976.

Him, along with a few hand picked soldiers he trusted, conducted raids and assassinations on Anti-American forces on the Island. The American Government, via the CIA, wanted the Rastas on the island to persuade the people to choose Capitalism

Awtuhm Duv: The Bird's Song

over the Socialistic policies that were in place. They knew, and Dez knew that the people, the poor people were being educated by and through the music.

This was the beginning of both his rise, and fall, as he upset the balance, haven killed one Rasa Zulu. They called him Jah-Zulu as he was not only warrior, but son of one of the highest Rastafari on the land.

Jah-Zulu was a rebel. He believed in the principles taught which consisted of being meek and alike. However, he had the heart of a lion, and fought endlessly against Dez, and his forces. Although the people from which he came didn't agree with his armed struggle, they understood. In the mountains is where he found his only refuge from battling day after day against Dez and his American supported associates.

They say Dez carried out the raids because, although they had the weapons, they couldn't overcome the will of the people and that the will was driven by the spirit of the meek people on the island in the mountains. So, they were sent to kill people at random in the mountains. Upon which, he either by accident or purpose cornered Jah-Zulu, taking his life. From

Awtuhm Duv: The Bird's Song

that day forth he was cursed. He knew he would have no peace for all his days had he remained on the island. Dez, once the part issued to him by the American government was carried out, found his path clear to the United States. He was openly banned as a trader, and couldn't obtain any legitimate position in the new Jamaican government.

Independence came to Jamaica. However, poverty was still king, as the violence was not altered by the changes. The fighting of youth against youth continued in the street like never before. The people were not fighting for the cause of politics. Rather, they had no jobs, and where just as hungry as before. Bodies would fall each day, as if a war was going on.

He, Dez, didn't much concern himself with the state of his people . He was more than well off financially. He dictated from the Mainland of America, and continued to distribute the weed by the boat loads. Bringing certain associates to America, and holding the 'better life' out of reach to them like a carrot. He would allow them to come and go forth to do his bidding. At the cost of being sent back to the island, they didn't quarrel with his position.

It wasn't only Zulu, but it was said that he attempted many other murders. Although many tried to rid the world of Dez, he was well protected. Not only did he have the man power, he was assisted with intelligence. From time to time he would pop up on the island, and just as suddenly disappear.

The spirit of Zulu never rested, lying, watching his every move, plotting its revenge. As high in the mountains of Jamaica the spirit was kept alive through a mystic prayer, and chants. Zulu's father and many of his people prayed, and wailed the end to Dez.

However, peace was holding a stronger hand, keeping reciprocity at bay through vibes and rhythms also created by the dreads. Just as there are more than one side to a coin. Even within the jungles of Jamaica there are differing views, and such was the case. Just as we have one government in America with different views. The Rasta on the island are one with differing views on handling business.

It was the view of the music man that kept the peace. For Rasta was just as well in the music. They say that the mystic

Awtuhm Duv: The Bird's Song

vibes of the rhythms kept evil from Dez, as peace was kept about him because those whom were injured by Dez didn't seek revenge. But only for a certain time. Then, just as sudden as calm and tolerable peace existed, it came to an end.

At first, it was whispered to be, the story of who he was and how all of this crime came about. How it all happened at first didn't seem as far fetched, especially when you feel it from the inside of you. Its like knowing something. You know, something that when it's said, sounds strange. But, it feels right. It feels like a perfectly fitting pair of new sneakers or a brand new swede jacket that raps about your arms, as if it is yours, made for you. You know it's yours, you have to have it, and not because you need it.

Hell, you don't even know you wanted it until you stumbled upon it. But just imagine if you met the person who made the jacket and they told you that they had a vision of you when they made the jacket, and they made it for you especially-having never met you before hand. That's how this story goes.

Awtuhm Duv: The Bird's Song

The Hit By Dez

It was the last time that Dez was ever seen on the Island of Jamaica. He had his soldiers carry out the plan. It was late one night as he watched from far off. The soldiers ambushed several people that night, killing many and wounding some. However, it didn't weaken the power of the mountains. In the carnage of it all, they missed the chief that chanted Dez's demise. Instead, they mistakenly murdered his other son, Jah-Zulu's brother. Now, not only did he have the blood of the priest's one son on his hands, he now also had another.

This son unlike Jah-Zulu was ordained to take the place of his father, the Chief Priest. He was majestic to his people. In that, he didn't fight for his father or on behalf of his people, he fought on behalf of the Almighty they said, and that made Dez appear as more trash than he was. As Dez was mocked as being a Yankee by the common folk, his name was not openly spoken on the island, and this infuriated him all the more..

Awtuhm Duv: The Bird's Song

On that night, they said the earth quaked, and the mountains thundered. They say that it was Zulu's spirit pushing the mountains from their place as he moved. Others say it was the strength of his father's soul seeking retribution. Only many knew what the rumblings were. It happens in all manner of living amongst people. The Lion, was in conflict with The Lamb. It was the roar of the Lion and it's having to be meek for a time still, as The Lamb had a bit more strength at the time. The strength was in the music, and in the power of one man, one music man soothing all the people and keeping life in balance. It wasn't time yet. But, that didn't stop Zulu's father from releasing his spirit for revenge.

It didn't matter the time. The curse was released into the air. It was only a matter of time that Zulu's warrior energy would seek out Dez. Upon not only Dez would retribution be had, but upon all his seed as well.

They say that Chief, Zulu's father never slept in a bed since Zulu's death, and fasted for times on end with ash upon his face ever since. So much so, people could only remember what he looked like, for no

Awtuhm Duv: The Bird's Song

one could see his skin. It was known to them, that he sat on the ground continuously, never allowing his body to leave the earth as to feel the footsteps of Dez. For years he chanted in hopes for the strength of his spirit to overpower the music. They claim that he would speak mumbling, then place his ear to the ground, listening for Dez and his footsteps. Many swear that when he spoke and muttered for hours at a time, that a steady stream of breath could be seen coming from his mouth as if he was in the winter weather of the far north. However on the island it was always summer.

Awtuhm Duv: The Bird's Song

The Cocaine

Dez had two sons even before he left the island. Although he never married the women who bore the boys, he brought them and their mothers with him to America. He had no loyalty to his country nor to any man or woman.

In 1980, he began in America a movement that most people in the industry would envy. He formed a partnership with other Carribean island thugs, as well as South American dealers. Since he had the import routes down to a science and the government continued to allow him to import weed. Dez took it to another level. He began to import cocaine via Jamaica. Without the government's permission or knowledge he began to become what is said to be the wealthiest dealer in the industry. He had the backing of the United States, and traveled back and forth to anywhere he wanted. This went on for a couple of years. He had the freedom to not only form alliances with the drug lords, he involved himself in weapons trafficking.

Awtuhm Duv: The Bird's Song

The peace that Dez was experiencing was not by his own thinking or doing. One of his victims, the music man's spirit kept harm from him, as the forgiveness of this one upon his soul was enough to fend off the curses attempting to lurch at the moments notice into his life.

Then, in 1981, it happened. Only five years after he thought he had escaped his past, it happened. That voice of peace was no longer and Dez's time was limited as bad fortune was to find him. The mist began to sense him and feel him out. The tides began to turn against him, and like a cold, sharp blade, it was to cut him.

Awtuhm Duv: The Bird's Song

DEZ In America

He was seeing a beautiful woman native to Jamaica at the time. She had two children as well. She had two girls and a mother she lived with. But, that didn't stop Dez. Her mother was from the old school, and felt a presence about Dez that made her feel nervous and uneasy. She was aware of the stories about him, but ignored the issue because it didn't effect her life as yet. Not only which, she was far from the plight of Jamaica. The money and the wealth was too much for her to comprehend. She remembered the old days in the 1960's in Jamaica and never knew of such a rich black man. As most mothers caring for her daughter, she sought out advice, and went to the soothsayer from the island, residing only blocks away.

She was a dark skinned woman, and had her hair rapped, and beads on the rap, around the long flowing gown and the staff she wielded. It was in the contacts with this other woman that the spirits far away on the island began to wax strong like a beacon. This woman not only knew of the past with Dez, she knew of his future, and passed that information onto the mother.

"Sure you know why you come mother," she stated at the opening of her door.

"Me Tears, Me Spirit."

"It is the time now. All know that."

"Oh Lawd. What? What me do?"

"Your daughter. Him seed, him life is cursed. Nothing can be done 'bout that now. You must rid him. When you grand baby first bleed come. Him must not be here. You must rid him."

"Oh, me tears," she wailed, as the smoke from the incense filled the air within the darkened room. She placed something in the dish at the door before exiting from the candle filled room. The eyes of the priestess was fixed to the back of the woman. Everyone knew who Dez was, and he couldn't simply be dealt with as the everyday man. This deed had to be done from the family, from someone close to him. He was too valuable to people and well protected. His fall meant the fall of many others.

The words of the soothsayer were to

come true as the woman told her daughter of the words. However, she was fascinated with the charms of Dez's wealth as the years went by, and she gave him a son and a daughter. Then, it came to past.

Awtuhm Duv: The Bird's Song

Blee and Slim Growing Up

We didn't have such an easy life growing up. But, things could have always been worst. Being a thug or gang member is only relevant to 'the activity'. We were gangster from the beginning, not knowing it.

When we were young we rolled in groups of ten or so, but it was about fun. It was practice for life. The things that happened in the mid to late seventies prepared us for everything. Forth grade is where it all happened, at age eight or so.

It didn't matter if we were friends sometimes. We had to fight. We had to jump the trains, and rob the neighbor's trees, and grape vines. We had to say: "fuck you," when they caught us in their yards, we had to run while we said that shit. Oh, and don't forget the middle finger.

If it wasn't nailed down we had a chance. We didn't steal like the crooks, we went on missions. We stole when we were hungry. Hunger, drives most everything in the world, and the fear of hunger, that makes it Raw. The Vietnam war was the only thing going on, and the recession. Whatever that was at the time.

Life was like it was suppose to be. Everyday you awoke, you had the same friends, people didn't move around all that much. Protecting our own, our territory was the call of the day. Gangs didn't just pop up. We started with the fake army men and all of the toy games, not to mention the boxing robots. Now a days, that's the cause of so many shootings in the streets, kids don't know how to fight with their hands. The first thing they get is a computer game and can't grasp and respect the value of life.

It wasn't a shock, our being in gangs as we got older. First, it was one block versus the other in football. Then, who had the best looking girls on their block. Not to mention, who parent or parents and neighbors had the cars, apartments, and houses or what have you.

On our block and the four or five other surrounding blocks, we developed an alliance. George was one of those leaders. He was smart. But, his real name was Jorge, he was part Puerto Rican. His sister

Carmen was fine as could be. I didn't know what it was though. She was fourteen, and the older guys thought that she was fine, so we thought she was fine.

Then, there was David, he was more of a Con. He was tall, fourteen years old and constantly in and out of reform or something. He just did shit. Usually, he would get caught stealing. Robert and Dennis were my favorites. Both of them were steady pains in the ass type niggas. They were always together and the biggest bullies. Their favorite lines were: "Why you looking at my sisters? If I catch you with my sister." Willette was her name, but we called her Gillette after the razor blades until she began to grow breasts. She was usually with Stephanie their cousin, and her cousin George.

The brothers didn't do school too much or too well. It was the place to get extra dough for them. Not that they needed it. Their father had the best of everything, and many women. Often, they would get nickels and dimes from children going to school or coming home for protection. The only way to avoid them would be to go the long way around the block or through the park down the boulevard. Even then, they would catch us at times.

 We didn't have such an easy life growing up. But, things could have always been worst. Sooner or later they would catch up with you and you'd have to pay up. Both Robert and Dennis had the same mother, same dad. His name was Dez. As I remember, he was hardly ever around. Their mother really didn't work. He paid the bills. Their father was all over the place, and their grandmother or some lady took care of them most of the time.

 Mrs. Perkins, their mother was never home, she worked three or four jobs we were lead to believe and usually was home during the day from eight in the morning or school time until right after school, or dinner. She would feed them and kick them out the house. Sometimes, she would kick them out even on Saturdays. She needed her rest because she had to be to work at her first job by four in the afternoon each day.

 Given the trouble her sons got into, Mrs. Perkins was never mean, or upset at the boys. Their father was another thing all together. They would argue and I couldn't understand what was being said. They were from the islands or somewhere.

Awtuhm Duv: The Bird's Song

I knew it was over women though, without a doubt. He loved the women. He stayed all over the place it was said. She was an attractive high-yellow woman with big booms, both ass and up top. Usually the fellas on the block would say: "Damn," or shook their heads and smile. Then came another boom of sorts. Her belly began to get bigger and the next thing you knew, their was suppose to be another addition to the family.

    Things didn't turn out quite that way. She had ended up missing one day. It was a Friday morning when no one seemed to see Robert and Dennis at their "jack" spot, robbing everyone. The relief for the day was taken in stride. No one was going to say that they actually missed getting robbed. It was like Christmas in the classroom. Everyone was talking about how they had all of their money. David even told about how he got tired of both of them taking his money and decided he had enough. So, he shot them and left them in the bushes at the back fence at the park. You didn't want to believe that it actually happened, but he had our attention. For the remainder of the day David(Blee) was our hero, and no one thought he had done anything wrong. At least he had the courage to kill them, we didn't.

The fact that there was going to be no more Robert and Dennis didn't bother anyone too much. We had enough of our getting slapped in the back of the head, and robbed. The nickle or dime each of us gave David that day was painless compared to the ones we had been taken for, for the past eight months since school started last fall. It meant that with those two brothers dead, we could go to the park and anywhere else we wanted to go during the upcoming summer.

We had collected almost eighty five cents that morning to give to David. He was going to show us the dead bodies in the bushes. But first, we promised not to tell anyone. No one would admit it but we were all scared. A couple of the kids didn't even want to go, even thought they had already pitched in. David told them that he would kill them too, had they said a word. Then, upon making it to the park, after not being able to concentrate during school, the pushing began when we got to the tall grass behind the park fence.

Cautiously, as we approached the area where David guided us toward the bodies, we started to jockey over last spot in the line as we pushed each other with the 'You First" thing. We started to trip over each other and slow, not wanting to really see them dead.

"Where are they?" David said, looking around.

"Yeah, Where the hell are they?" Marquis said as his eyebrows came together.

"The Police, I think they found them. Hey, y'all can't tell no one. Alright? I have to hide out until everything is clear." David said convincingly.

"Where, where you gonna hide out?' I asked him.

"First, I gotta go home and get rid of the gun. That's the first place they will look, because someone might have seen me. Then, I have to get some food and some more money in case I have to get away."

"My mother went shopping last night," Joey said.

"Puerto Rican food?"

"What you mean?"

"Shit, we got American food. It's from America. It ain't Puerto Rican until you make dinner."

"Good, good," David whispered, placing his arm around Joey's shoulder. "You go home and make some sandwiches or something and I'll try to find a place to hideout until then. I'll be at your back door at about five if they don't catch on to me. If the news don't say anything you come to the 'way back' part of the backyard and let me know. That's where I'll hide out. Everybody." Dave looked around like we had a secret.

"You all watch T.V. news and let Marquis know. You watch channel eight," pointing at me, "you watch channel 11," pointing at Marquis, "and you watch channel four," whispering at Jose, leaning in and putting his finger to his chest.

    We all had each other's telephone numbers. We ran from the park pathway, which was just about thirty feet from the street. As we scattered, I was sure that everyone's heart was racing just as mine was. Unlike most of the children in my class, I had not only brother and sisters at home, I had both parents. Chores had to be done 'or else'. The 'or else' meant a definite ass beating when dad got home.

    The only concern I had was getting in front of the television. That was no problem because that's what my parents did each evening after dinner. I made sure my homework was done in record time. I wanted to hear about the dead bodies found at the park. I never knew anyone famous before. I didn't think that I'd ever see anyone I knew on television. Just like a cat closing in patiently on a mouse, I sat at the foot of my mother's bed on the floor. "At the top of the news tonight," the reporter started. "We have just learned of a gruesome discovery in the Woodhill community, as neighbors are stunned." That was us I thought. David wasn't lying. He killed them, as my eyes got big. While the lump in my throat made it's way down. "A tragedy has occurred. We mourn the lives of two innocent people today. A woman and her unborn child was found who's name is believed to be that of Aretha Perkins and an unborn child believed to be four months. The body of Mrs. Perkins was found, apparently shot to death in a parked car early this morning at about five thirty, outside of a nightclub. Police are still investigating and looking for the perpetrator. It is known that she worked at the club. Reports are sketchy at this time. But, we are sure to have more in

Awtuhm Duv. The Bird's Song

the investigation of this tragedy later tonight. Mrs Perkins is survived by two sons."

The gossip in the community was that she worked at the club, owned by Dez, and was sleeping with one of the men that either worked or frequented the club. Some say that the baby was the other guys baby. Some say that the other guy murdered her because if Dez found out that the baby was his, he was done. Others believe Dez did the deed because she told him the baby was not his, and she didn't want him in her life anymore. No matter the case, she was gone.

My mother and father were in shock to see Mrs. Perkins face on our television. I never knew anyone that was in the television before. It wasn't Robert or Dennis, and although it may seem cruel looking back. She filled my need to have seen someone I knew on televison.

I had just seen her a couple of days ago, and there she was, her picture on the television. I felt sad that it was her. Then, my mind shifted to it not being Robert and Dennis. David had played all of us. But that didn't matter. "Poor kids," my mother said. The joy of Robert and Dennis being alive came over me.

  We all met up in Marquis's backyard at the far end, all of us except David. He had come for the sandwiches and left. We knew we were taken in again. We all agreed on one thing though, we were glad that it was David that lied and not us. We also knew if Dennis and Robert found out, that was his ass.

The Funeral

I never had the opportunity to see a dead body before. Not only which, one that I actually saw walking before. My mother went to the funeral and I begged her to let me go. I had went over to Robert's and Dennis's house before the funeral with my parents to pay respect. Their aunt was there receiving guests and eventually moved in with them, and their grandmother. The aunt had two girls: Willette and Steph. She also had a boyfriend.

Steph was only about ten years old when I first met her, and Willette was a couple years older. We became friends of sorts as I like-liked Willette, especially in the next year or so as her body got bigger. Neither of them were smart so to speak. I wanted Willette, and the only way I could get any time was by seeing her younger sister. We did homework together.

This went on for a couple of years until Willette met one of Steph's cousins and made me cry. Even though George was

Steph's cousin, he and Willette weren't related. They would walk and hold hands, and sit and watch television. It was then, I decided not to go around too much longer. My heart couldn't take anymore. I guess that's why they call it a 'crush', because my heart was without a doubt crushed.

Robert and Dennis became totally different. They had mustaches, and didn't really have time to beat us up anymore. Their aunt didn't make them do anything, and to tell the truth, they were hardly ever around. They were following their father most of the time.

Robert and Dennis found out that their aunt was working for the same cat at the club that their mother worked at, and that her boyfriend was her pimp or something. Needless to say, that was the end of it, the relationship between her and her boyfriend. They found out also that the man was pimpin' their mother. Too make it worst, he was later said to be the father of Mrs. Perkins unborn child.

Then, lightening seemed to have struck twice. The dude was found in his car in the same parking lot as Mrs. Perkins. He had his head blown off they say. No one ever

Awtuhm Duv. The Bird's Song

knew who did either murder. It wasn't long after that Dez started to sleep with Steph and Willette's mother, who was his dead wife's sister. This, against the advice of the grandmother, who warned her. It was her mother, not his. She felt her other daughter would be next.

The mother warned her daughter, and it was then that she told her daughter about the curse. The grandmother brought her daughter to see the priestess. The daughter wasn't blind to the rumors, and heard of the things that Dez had done while back home in Jamaica. It had become too late for her. She couldn't resist Dez.

The person was dreaded. With a long cloak on and beads, she could hardly be told from a man except for when she spoke in her smoke filled room, a dark room. "You must leave child. Take your girls. He will have the one and not the other. His seed is cursed. Get your girls out of there before the second daughter bleeds her first bleed. Whatever that man touches will turn to shit. He is cursed from the mountains and the seas." That's all the warning she was given. It was similar to that of the woman before, the one that the grandmother saw a few years ago.

It wasn't long before a cloud came over that house. It was even sooner that she found herself pregnant. Just like her sister, she began to drink and smoke. She had given birth to a baby boy. Then, she was pregnant with a second child, and gave birth. Steph was now turning twelve.

Willette was fifteen or so and was dating Cuz, as before. They had been seeing each other in private on occasion, and they were both ready to take their relationship to another level. But, it wasn't to be so, not yet. During the spring, one night during the rain, the guidance of the woman came to past.

As the lightening cracked and the air was in turmoil, Willette was in her room and sleeping, dreaming of Cuz. She had never been with a man. But, she could feel him as her body began to give way to pleasure and desire in her sleep as she could feel Cuz loving her.

At the very same moment, Steph was unknowingly having her first period. She was to wake up the following morning in shame, as her night clothes were bloodied. It was not the same shame for Willette. Dez had come into Willette's room while she slept, and dreamed. From under the bottom parts of the bed he watched her have dreams and no sooner had he sensed her wanting, he began bringing the warnings to truth. He slid under the cover like the snake he was and began to lick in between her legs. Only, she didn't know the difference between what she was dreaming and what she was feeling as her body began to convulse, and just as quickly Dez slid into her as her eyes opened. She didn't know any better, she thought she did it. She thought she wanted it, and they continued, as it was that night she conceived his child.

Not long after that, Stacy, Willette's mother started to fade. She had a terrible toll on her spirit. Suddenly, she started to use drugs. To add to the sense of feeling helpless having given Dez two children and to see her daughter pregnant by him as well. She tried to hide from the fact that Willette was going to become a mother. The grandmother sensed that it was Dez who did it. However, Willette had begun to sleep with Cuz, and he claimed the deed as his own. Stacy could feel it. She felt to the bone the words of the wise woman, and so did the grandmother.

With all of the pain, they went to the

hospital the night Willette had given birth and took the baby from her. Cuz was told that the baby was still born. However, the mother and grandmother knowing the truth, convinced Willette to give the baby up for adoption. They managed to get her to see that it was Dez's baby. It was said to look just like him and the babies her mother had with him.

The mother's burden became terrible, as she at times let her other sister watch the younger children. She constantly drank and smoked weed, and then she began with the cocaine. Willette began to spend more time at Cuz's house, not wanting to be around Dez. But, Dez was a low rat of a man. He allowed his younger children's mother to get as high as she wanted. This allowed her sister to take care of their babies together.

He would go over late at night to pick them up and bring them home. Sometimes they stayed with their aunt. He liked the way she wore her night shirts as he drooled like a dog at her. She was only about five feet five inches tall. But, she was well built, and had one son. He made plays on her, and finally she gave in.

She began to see the downfall of her

sister, and wanted what Stacy had. She thought it to be a perfect opportunity to win over Dez from her sister, not realizing he was no prize. Dez had all the things in life anyone could ask for. He had several women, cars, and babies, and took care of all of them, lovely. Then one night he stopped by unannounced.

"What you want? You said the kids were spending the night. They are asleep Dez."

"I know."

"You know, so why you here?" Already knowing why, and wanting the same thing.

"You know."

"I know what?"

"You know you want me girl. Look at you and that almost nothing on. Stop playing," as he grabbed her. She didn't budge.

"You know you wrong Dez."

"Stop playing girl," as he lifted her shirt to see the rest of her.

"Not out here," she brought him into the bedroom and lit some candles. The children had been asleep for an hour or so. She made sure to have fed them late, and let them play 'til exhaustion.

Turning on the music, she then undressed Dez and went to her knees unbuckling his pants, taking him into her mouth.

Holding him and licking, she began to ask: "You gonna treat me right?" as all he could do is moan for her. She knew that her sister didn't do these things for Dez, because of the many women he had. She didn't care, she went all out. Her drive was not wanting Dez, but the endless bank he had. She wanted to give him a baby too. Dez took care of his babies, if not the women in his life. Financially he cared for the women, but he didn't have a heart for them.

    She lifted him and began to pull on his nuts until he couldn't take it anymore. All he could say was "Yeah baby." She had him to his back on the bed and straddled him with her ass facing him as he clutched her ass. It was firm and shapely.

"You like that baby?"

"Oh yeah."

"Spank mama," as he slapped her firmly.

    "Like that baby," she moaned as her lips parted and her tongue went across the lower lip and she bent over even more, readjusting herself, looking back at him.

"Put your thumb in my ass," she moaned

and he obliged.

"You's a freaky momma ain't you," she went up and down and he began to thrust harder upward as he saw the look of joy and pain on her face. Getting to his knees he kept his thumb in place as he came up from behind her, stroking her until her head dropped to the bed as she screamed into the mattress.

"This what you wanted all along bitch," as he spanked her and then finally he came. It wasn't over to say the least. She began to suck him off some more until he came around again, and this time she faced him, riding him until the next one came, and then again, until he passed out into a coma-like state.

After Affects

Nine months had passed and Stacy's sister had the baby for Dez. She told everyone that the baby was for someone else, but people could sense otherwise. It was dirty, but Dez was dirty. Eventually she told Stacy the truth, and Stacy graduated to crack. She started to see things and became delusional. Not long after, she was committed to an institution for a program.
 "Your momma ain't here no more, and your grandma moved out. I guess you the Queen now Willette," Robert said. The grandmother couldn't take anymore of the stresses. She felt the shame of the situation, and moved into her own place. Dez moved into the place with Stacy's sister, and she took care of Stacy's smaller two children with her aunt. They called her Mama Auntie.
 "I'm the Queen," Steph said.
 "No, she's older. She has to watch out for you, Tray said so."
 "Tray? Who the hell is Tray?"

"Dennis, and don't start bugging."

"Well, who the fuck is you?" Steph looked at Robert with her eyes wide open and her hands on her hips. "If you don't mind," looking at Queen, swiveling her neck, looking at him from the corner of her eyes.

"Ragga," he said, as the girls laughed at him.

"Ragga?" Steph covered her mouth laughing with Queen.

"Ragga? Wait, wait. Who the hell is this?" Pointing at Steph.

"I'm Big Steph from the east side," as she started to mimic signs from different gangs, holding a B-Boy stance and laughing. "I'm the queen?"

"Big Steph is in charge over everything right? Shit, I am B-I-G Steph right Robert? I mean, Ragga," as he smiled.

"Please, ain't nothing higher than the Queen," as she pushed by Steph not having to.

Then, Tray came through the door.

"Yo Tray! What up my nig?" as Queen tried to give him some palm.

"Yo, go 'head Will."

"Will? I'm Queen. You ain't tell this nigga?" Looking at Ragga.

"Yeah, Yeah"
"I'm Big Steph."
"Look, whoever the fuck y'all are now. You got to be holding shit down in here. I don't want niggas up in this bitch okay. No more of that bullshit, for real! You heard Queen? BabyGirl?" As they both sucked their teeth in understanding.

"What up bro-?"
"Pop is locked the fuck up now. That means shit changes. You know?"

"Word?"
"You know," Tray tried to keep the conversation tight.

I was only thirteen by now, and since that day. I wasn't allowed to just pop up around the crib anymore. No one was allowed in the house. Not George or anyone. Queen and BabyGirl stayed at home and when they went to school and came home, George took them, he dropped out a while back.

Dez got popped for the importation of narcotics. It appeared that the government found out that he had cocaine interest and they wanted to control that aspect of his business. Jail has a way of getting a person's attention. It was only suppose to be a small bump in the road. It was a means for the government to re-negotiate with him. Taking him off the streets was the trick they would use to get his attention. It was said he was found at the harbor with some out of country niggas trying to get two hundred kilos from under a ship docked at port.

Things Change

    Tray and Ragga had no time for the bullshit anymore. They didn't even speak to us, but they didn't fuck with us either. We saw them everyday now, just the same. Only thing is, they began to hang with these other cats. Most times they ignored us. Sometimes they were with brothers I never seen before. Most of the guys were older and had cars. I could only recognize them, and Cuz in the crowd. A few of the others were their father's peoples. Time pasted and things got more intense as niggas was warring over blocks and spots. There were never these types of disputes before. However, when crack came along things changed.
    It became an entirely different breed of people on our streets now. They were not Puerto Rican- Puerto Ricans, they were Cuban, Columbians and all types, and they made it known that they weren't Puerto Ricans. Dez imported them with the cocaine he started to bring in. Things moved faster, and the neighborhood went down the tubes from there as mafuckas

Awtuhm Duv: The Bird's Song

began to steal like crazy to get hits from the pipe. Not to mention all of the shootings, shootings just for the sake of shooting.

    Queen was a woman and Steph was almost there. They were as good as grown in the brain, and Queen was still seeing Cuz. Steph was seeing some other cat, but not for real though. Ragga put a stop to all of that. But Queen, she and Cuz was a bit more serious, and Ragga had left them alone, They were a part of the crew. Tray, he didn't care much for Cuz. Cuz was a playa just like him. Cuz never disrespected Queen to her face. But, she had beef with a lot of those, 'He say, She say' chicks. Tray didn't like shit that got in the way of business, quickly putting an end to Cuz's ways.

    Prosperity began to come to an end for Dez. He was implicated in one of the biggest drug busts in the country. It wasn't for the marijuana. Cocaine took him to jail. That was the means the United States used to get him off the streets and to hide prior deals they permitted with the weed. He would have been straight as long as he dealt with the weed. He messed up when he used the routes he used to smuggle the weed from the island for those South American cats smuggling shit in through the island and then to Miami.

He was fine, until he didn't cut the big boys in on the take. They knew he was making the big dollars from cocaine. What probably happened was that those South American cats did cut the dirty handlers in and ratted him out. That is what jail was for. It gave the lawyers a chance to shake down money from clients and transfer assets, and re-establish agreements. That's all it was to Dez. Putting him behind bars made him more accessible. He could hear a little better after they took away the power he wielded. It would have been senseless to send him back to Jamaica. He would have probably ended up in Europe.

They couldn't explain that which they didn't know. He got greedy and even worst. Stacy got out of rehabilitation. She wasn't as crazy anymore. She listened the next time her mother brought her to the wise woman.
"You go and love that man. You go and hate that man," she was told, whatever that meant at the time. This time, it was the first woman the mother had gone to.

Although she wasn't able to have anymore children. The deed was on her. It wasn't long before the heaviness was placed in her heart, although she had forgotten about having Dez in her life, she knew that he had to go. As a mother, she hated him for what he did with her oldest daughter.

Their younger son together, had come down with the flu and then died a month later with pneumonia, and other complications. It was said that upon the child's passing, the same priestess was outside of the hospital window watching and waiting for his spirit. That very night, the chief was on the island calling for the child's spirit as well, not yet satisfied.

Her mother didn't make situations better. She would constantly release whisperings against Dez. Her mother would whisper things to her, and she began to believe that Dez was a curse to her and her babies.

"Him sleep with you daughter, and with you sister. Him sleep with both me daughters, and me grand. Him wife dead, him baby dead. My grand dead. My grand will dead. Both my daughters have him babies, and me grand have him baby," she constantly moaned, motivating Stacy.

No matter, she couldn't save the children. Her mother knew that, but she never told her.

Awtuhm Duv: The Bird's Song

Thinking that she could save her older child, she listened to the words of the woman, and began to correspond with Dez, and then she began to see him. She pretended the love as the soothsayer advised. Dez, being lonely and such as a nigga could be in jail, began to take her visits from the prison, and then they began open visits. It was at this time the wise woman passed on to Stacy's mother the potion to handle Dez.

It was with a kiss at the visit that Stacy gave Dez a piece of chewing gum laced with something that sealed his fate. He chewed the gum that night before he went to sleep as he called Stacy. They say he seized up in the corridor. Her mother was standing by just as attentive as a doctor carefully listening for a heartbeat. The mother grabbed the phone from Stacy. "Let me hear, let me hear." As she listened to his last breaths. It was done and the older woman breathed a sigh of satisfaction, and the priestess chanted and The Chief on the Island smiled and with laughter reached for the heavens. For now, it was done.

They shipped the body back to Jamaica. There, Jah-Zulu's father waited, and they say he plucked the eyes from Dez's corpse. Then, later that night in the mountains, he wished the eyes of Dez's children, as he burnt Dez's eyes and danced. Finally, he was able to take a bed and sleep, and rest after all of those years of making the ground his home, listening to Dez's footsteps in the distance. After all of those years, he washed and came clean, and for the first time in a long time people saw his face, and hailed him. In his lying down and even in his sleep that night he smiled and laughed. He smiled.

Awtuhm Duv: The Bird's Song

Stacy with Sister after Dez

It wasn't long after Dez was buried before Stacy began to look, feel and act better, as she came to her senses. She became the person she once was before Dez.
"So, you wanted what I have?" she asked her sister, as she circled her sister. This was the first conversation they had had in some time. Neither knew if it was about to come to blows or not. Without notice, she broke into a smile. Stacy was oldest, and finally after years of torment she let her sister know.
 "You have no idea do you? Shit, any other man, and I wouldn't care as much. But, you are my sister and I would never wish this upon you. Hell, not even my enemy."
 "He's dead now. Let it go," her sister replied, sucking her teeth and rolling her eyes.
  "He was a curse, and so too his seed. There ain't no letting it go. When can you let go of your baby? " She began to remember all of the things that Dez did since meeting her, and all of the women, as

tears filled her eyes.

"You don't want this, and you have no idea what 'this' is. Usually.........," as she sniffled. "Usually sisters talk about the man that they are going with or gonna be with. He even took that away. We didn't even have that. I mean, I shared my pains with you, but you used it to take my man, or should I say everyone's man. You would of thought that knowing what I was going through that you wouldn't want it. Did you know that Queen's baby was his baby?" Her sister's mouth dropped and she began to sob, and sniffle along with Stacy.

"Hell, I wouldn't have told you but since you are in the same boat with the rest of us, you may as well know. Welcome to the party. Now, you have what we have," throwing up her arms, and letting them drop, while shaking her head, trying to laugh through the tears. .

Stacy tried to tell her sister, but she couldn't see because of what Dez left her with. She had a house and everything.

"Maybe you are wrong," as she wiped her tears, and sat back.
"You'll regret that nigga before it's over with."

"Look, you're just upset because he wanted me and not you."

"No, I am upset that I care for you and you don't give a damn about yourself, nor your baby. I don't know what's gonna happen to mine. But, hey, keep your eyes open."

Stacy wasn't upset. She was disappointed as she left. Walking down the steps, she began to wonder just how bad this was going to get.

Later

The block was always held down by at least ten brothers or more. A couple of the fellas had spoiler kit type shit on their wheels. Other brothers didn't floss like that. Ragga and Tray had a whole lot of dough. They were in charge now, and they learned enough from Dez. They played it like they had no dough. Not one person knew where Dez put all that cash. Some said that Ragga had it. Some said that Tray had it.

    One day, shit happened. Out of nowhere, RAWGA popped up. We were all just sitting and doing what we did. Niggas had no idea what was going on. But Tray and Ragga went ill with these grills nobody ever seen before. They were identical in name. The letterings were in different places. No one knew what it meant. No matter, shit got contagious.

    Cuz and some members of the crew became jealous. Other brothers in the crew went out and got plates, knuckles, and vanity tags with RAWGA on them. The name was off the hook. Brothers from here to there knew of the name, and at the same time no one but the two brothers knew what it was about. They never spoke of it either.

    RAWGA is what made Tray and Ragga the chiefs and the others Indians. From that day on, cats would come to them for advice and answers. Then one day, it all fell into place. Tray and Ragga left the block and started calling the shots. There was no more of the diplomacy type conversations. They thought up a plan on how to expand and spend the dough they were stacking. All of the old cats from Dez crew fell in line as well. It was them that bridged the gaps in the connections that Dez had, and it was a new influx in blood. The older cats allowed their youth to join up with Tray and Ragga, as they themselves did with Dez.

Just as quick as it happened, so did other things. Houses were being bought and the bosses took with them the brotha's that were down. Others, got rolled on, and over. The members that bit off of Tray and Ragga were given dogs, and were organized into groups. They came and left the block.

Cuz, since he liked the women, was made captain on the block. Eventually, he went RAWGA but he did so to stick out his chest. He didn't have the true type pride in it. He was just in it to floss. The shameful thing was that one crew cat got his grill done, which showed no respect. Not that he was disrespecting Tray and Ragga, you can say that he didn't know the rules and got carried away with shit. There's always some shit like this. The next thing anyone knew, some brothas busted and kicked his teeth in, causing his jaw to need wiring. No one knew who it was that did it. He still had a job. Some didn't understand why whomever did that shit just didn't tell him to take them shits out. The nigga should have known better......period.

Awtuhm Duv. The Bird's Song

From my perspective, he should have known better. But then, one day, both Ragga and Tray showed up with these Diamond and Gold permanent RAWGA in the grill. From that day on, no one got any knuckles or anything done with Rawga on it without permission. That part was made apparent when a cross town cat was sprayed because he got a shirt made up with the name RAWGA on it. He didn't have the shirt on when he got hit. He didn't much draw his last breath either. But, he never wore that joint again. His brother brought the shirt to the block one day, and that was that.

Me and David, we would hustle a bit on our own. He'd call me Slim and I called him Blee. He wasn't as close to Tray and Ragga as when we were kids getting jacked everyday. He had his own style and his own ways of getting paid. He mimicked them brotha's and wasn't scared of shit. The crew didn't have to respect us, we were small fry. But, we knew what was going on in the 'hood.

We could only get enough paper to say we were trying to do something. Everything came back to RAWGA. We would find weed for people who didn't know better, and sometimes powder. People would come to us and we would act like we knew where to get the shit. We just never told them that we weren't apart of the crew. We rolled some, and others we maintained. We would hit-up the weed bags until we got enough for our own blunt, and shit like that.

I got In

It was a surprise to me that I made it into the crew. I never found out who nominated me, and I really didn't care. The only thing different about things is that I could no longer hang out and do 'just' nothing with Blee. We remained friends, and spent time bull-shitting around. But, usually my days were all mapped out.

The first of my jobs was easy. On the first day of things I had to watch. I watched cars, and customers. Mostly, I had to watch for the police. Then, I had to run to the store for the crew. It didn't matter what they needed. If the order wasn't right, I had to go back for more or different shit. I guess it was paying dues.

Then, I was allowed to carry my first piece of steel. It was like power, the way it felt in my hand, heavier than it appeared to be. It made me feel strong at first, and then when I would see the other cats stuff, I felt scared. They might fuck around and pull the trigger on accident I thought.

"Ever shoot one of them shits?" One of

the members asked.

"What the fuck you think?" No sooner had I pulled the clip and started to check out the barrel, they took it from me.

I helped my father clean his weapons all the time. The only difference is, I was cleaning them to hunt or protect the house. Out there, on the block, I felt like I was ready to actually use one. I shot a gun a few times, only not at people.

"Here, you hold on to this," they gave me a .380. Then, my head began to scan the street with purpose. I could actually hit someone. I was waiting for the night time to come.

Later that night, at about seven or so, I was given a bundle. It was my first bundle, and not even five minutes later I had made my first sale. I was officially a member of the crew. With that honor or dishonor came my first blunt. I had no idea how to approach the situation. Me and Blee were smoking all the while. I never smoked with anyone but him.

I felt a sense of being out of place, we usually did certain shit when we smoked. Niggas got mad because I wouldn't smoke with them. I rolled my own shit, and stepped off to myself. I didn't know them brothas like that. A couple of them I didn'tcare for me or my style, they were some booty cats out their. They ain't like the brothas Ragga and Tray ran with a few years back, and even before Tray and Ragga, there were cats on the block. Dez had this sowed up for years. I didn't want to be part of them niggas lives, just part of the crew. Some of those cats were just stupid, ignorant mafuckas.

<u>Me Tears</u>

The Stab

The days became pretty much the same.
"Yo' man. Can you front me a little something?" Customers or Custies is what we called the base heads, would ask.
"Them the niggas you wanna see muthafucka. {pointing down the block}. We don't do no shit like that. You betta get the fuck up from 'round here with that bullshit, I'd tell them.
"We get money nigga, that's it bitch. Carry yo' ass on." My partner finished, turning his back and spitting on the ground, trying to get to the next customer money.
We just didn't do no shit like that, that credit shit. It feels like the brotha, even though he didn't mean to, disrespected us. Even if that wasn't the case and all with the disrespect. We ain't in the business where you can actually have people questioning what the hell is going on down the block. The Establishment held markers. That was their end.
They never held any weight. They had

Me Tears

their own shit. They kept eyes from that point of the block. They never took paper; not on our block. Shit went out, not in. They never handed off shit directly either. Them dogs worked for them. Brothas never wanted to see the dogs not coming. They did shit on account.

Marks, that's what we called the Stab clients. You had to be getting checks to be a mark. The plan was set in play by application and that only. First, they had to have an address for collection. The niggas didn't play that 'bring shit' crap. At that address, the place where you set up the account, is where you paid. Not at the corner store or no park, or no bullshit like that. Muthafuckas settled tabs on dates, times, and places. Each Mark had a date, time and place. If your ass got paid on Friday, that was your date....pay day. The dogs walked their ass off all fucking evening on Friday. You never seen dogs walk as much as them pits, and rots. They were like hunting niggas 'cause that's what they were doing, only on chains and leashes.

The rules were as such that you couldn't cop before you settled up. Even more strange is the fact that a Mark

<u>Me Tears</u>

couldn't pay for shit the same night he settled up. The Mark had to come and get credit, and it didn't matter if he or she had dough. Their money was never any good on the block. One step further, if the Marks for some reason couldn't score, they definitely couldn't visit our ass on the other end either. We just couldn't fuck with Marks, that lost came out of our pockets or our ass. It was just a lose-lose situation to fuck with Stab Marks. Those in the crew that were stupid enough to run scam like that usually got missing for a minute, and most of the time came back to work limping, bruised, all depending. Sometimes, they didn't make it back, all depending.

    You created problems for the Stab by dishing shit to a Mark. That meant nonsense, and that meant your ass was in play. For real, I saw a pit just holding on to a nigga's ass while one of them Stab brotha's re-established the rules. Blood was coming out through the nigga's jeans and all. The brotha was actually crying and everything. Thank God the dog wasn't told to shake or rip a piece out of his ass. He just held him there. The brother later said he was scared to bend because the

Me Tears

other 'pit' may have grabbed his throat. Although things could have been worst for the brotha, he only ended up with bandage type shit wrong with him, which was peace. Nigga don't need spike chew-chewing on your ass. The fact that Marks were explained the rules by the Stab created less frictions.

 Marks came in all type, and in all fashion. One thing, you couldn't be was a welfare patient and open an account with the Stab. The Boss didn't go for that shit. If you needed assistance from the state, you needed not to use in the first. We called them niggas 'ghosts' because they could only see us at night. Welfare patients, we didn't like them around during the day. Too much heat.

 All Marks had homes and cars. We even knew where they worked. We had people for them too. Queen and Steph were the only ones allowed to visit jobs. They handled Stab business on that end. Collecting is what they did on the high end. They had business, and were in all phases of shit going on. You couldn't recognize them for the shit they sported.

 The suits they sported were in the 'G' money. They had brief cases at times, and

<u>Me Tears</u>

the whole get-up. Those clients, they didn't take home visits. They lived on the other side.

Me Tears

The Other Side

That's where the grass is greener-for'il. That's where Queen and Steph lived most of the time. They were true pimps in the business. All of those high end clientele like the Bankers, Lawyers, Doctors, you name it. Male or female were served by Big Steph and The Queen. They had a stable of about fifty broads, of all types. If you were a man wanting action, you had to go to Steph or Queen from the uptown. But, the main thing was the weight. It didn't matter who the Mark was for them, they eventually became clients of the Stab. Once someone, anyone went from just wanting to get a paid piece of ass, to wanting product, they were referred to Stab.

If you saw the ass on these chicks Queen brought by you'd get the understanding. People don't understand. Pussy, that gets a brothas attention. Drugs, that gets into bank accounts. It didn't only apply to brotha's. We had women who wanted some 'man'.

Me Tears

Sometimes Queen and Steph would ride up on us and tell a crew cat: "get the fuck in the car," and brothas didn't say shit. It didn't matter if you had a wife or not. It was a part of the job. They got paper, sometimes G-money a nut. The worst part is that it could be a Black, White, Hispanic, fat, wrinkly, old, stink piece of pussy. We never knew.

Then, they had brothas just for tricking too, dick down niggas is what we called them. They thought they were better than us because they didn't work the block, but we couldn't really fuck with them either, although they were nothing but punks. Queen and Steph didn't like none of us fucking with their money makers like that. Some of them went from being 'get-high' niggas themselves, to respectable- working- 'get high' niggas. Of course, some got caught up in the moment and were just tricks, just like a street whore selling their bodies for crack. I never had anything against a street hustle. But, I always thought the female tricks had it better sucking these dirty dicks than a brother licking some dirty cunt. That's just my opinion.

The ass on some of Queen and Steph's

Me Tears

chicks would make any brotha grunt, and say: "damn." Eventually, all those brothas were gonna get a pipe pushed in their mouth or a straw up their noses by these tricks. They didn't work weed because it wasn't good business, and each time one of their clients asked, they told them they needed a hit of powder even if they didn't use. They would have them buy the shit, and keep it, like a tip for later.

"I wanna do you right first," they would tell these stupid ass fathers, doctors, lawyers or what have you. When the client said "Lets do it together," that was mission complete. If the trick didn't get high, she would fake the sniffing shit. The next thing they did, they sent in a get high, freak-pro, for the power move. Besides, a brotha could sniff an eight-ball, or smoke an ounce of crack while two niggas could get right from a spliff, and that weed just wasn't profitable. We didn't want to relax niggas, we wanted them to put on the high beams, so they couldn't see.

Dope was out of the question. Not one person did dope. The rocks was the "it". This business was just that. The store only opened on Friday and Saturday. The girls in the stable worked only two nights a

Me Tears

week. They all got ready on Thursday. This meant nails and hair, and shopping. Most of the girls had regular type jobs during the week. Ass got kicked if they were ever caught playing on The Other Side with a Mark during the other parts of the week. Queen, and Steph were really serious about that type shit. Queen, and Steph would let them know that all those men were their husbands and that those bitches could only fuck their husbands when they said they could. Their husbands couldn't be out fucking all week. They had to work during the week, just like married people, and the tricks were the means to get the chedda'.

"You can't milk a cow all damn day, let the heffa eat and rest, then milk it," Queen would say.

The beauty shop was owned an operated by Queen and Steph too. Steph was into the hair fashion thing. We got our cuts free, and all the members had regular appointments. It is probably the only place I ever saw that did so much hair grooming and money was never any good there. The only problem was sitting their and waiting and watching the women.

First, the chicks would sit there talking.

Me Tears

Then, they would start reading. Then, they would start reading and talking at the same time. This, while someone was putting what would amount to be lye, and some other shit to the scalp of a woman, which turned their hair a whole different color. The color was always different from what hair should look like.

    Regular people never went there because you could wait, and wait forever because a crew member from the block or wherever in the organization would just come in and be next. When the barber says: "Yo, he was next," and you sat there all that time there's nothing you can do. Just to make a stupid ass feel better someone might say that the member called earlier. Usually the Stab, Them Niggas, and The Bosses got their shit done on Thursdays. Thursdays were the nights that new clientele were entertained.

    The spot to be was Spot 3. We called it that because it was the third spot that people in the crew knew about. It was the only spot that you could be welcomed into and not worry about getting shot. It was our own spot, our club. The women, after getting all did-up would come down to the spot to show their appreciation to the

<u>Me Tears</u>

Bosses, and at the same time tune up for Fridays and Saturdays. Nothing seriously went on during the evening.

The party always ended when Queen, and them left which was early, about eleven at the latest. They needed their rest for the weekend. Sometimes, depending on, if a crew member did something good in business that week, or if family died or some shit like that, one of the girls would hit us off in the bathroom or outback. The best was having to give one of them a ride home.

It was the best night for us because we could sit back and watch the chicks get the potential new Marks hot, which got us hot, which I know they were hot. They just couldn't give them any, and because it was a working night, the next night, it was like live porn. The Stab was in the house like fast food counter people taking orders on a Saturday night after a high school football game. Then, just as sudden as they appeared, the girls would leave.

Just because these cats were invited didn't mean they would be given an account either. They were only prospects for the most part. The majority were referred by Marks anyhow, and they had to

Me Tears

come up with the names of the Mark that referred them. Then, employment had to be verified, and then when the Mark who referred the prospect paid on his tab the next day, he or she had to personally vouch for the prospect. It may seem to be a lot. But, applications were done in one business day. The most important thing about Thursday night was the getting of numbers from the prospect.

They had the women, or men of their dream the next night if things went well, and that's when phase one kicked in. This is when the prospects were given what we call the 'pussy' rules. Then, when they paid the tab the following Friday, they were given the rest of the rules by the Stab. The humorous thing about it was that most Marks didn't even care to know the other rules concerning 'base', or what-have-you. They just wanted to get laid. Then one day eventually the chicks would turn them into powder sniffing, or crack heads, and then the line would be: "Do you remember what you said about......," they would say. It works, ching-ching.

If I had a nickel for all of the clients that eventually swore that they fell in love with one of the workers, I would retire.

Me Tears

Ragga wasn't about having a nigga fall in love with the ladies. It was business. We called it 'ball in love' because the sorry mafuckas would cry over these bitches, and beg to have certain ones. It was pathetic. The women were there for just the new clients. Old clients were serviced away from the spot. We couldn't fall in love with them either. He kept the list and chicks went to where he sent them. Shit was so tight, you thought it was take-out. Whatever the weight, height, color, and everything was asked just to make people happy.

    Ragga had better not find out that any of us were fuckin' his wives during the week either. He didn't like that shit. I could only imagine that is where Queen got the concept. Ragga took shit personally. He had women that did certain things too. All of his women did different things, and he had some that did everything. Some of them would use contraptions of all types. Some of the men, Queens husbands so to speak, liked the women to fuck them up the ass. Some of them like to fuck the women in the ass. That was some expensive shit I heard. The freakier, the more it costs. The freakier, the better.

<u>Me Tears</u>

The freakier, the more cocaine they needed. The smooth thing about it for the women was that once the Stab took an order, the women would harass Queen and Steph for the assignment of clients. They were some freaky tricks themselves, don't be fooled. You couldn't knock them for getting paid for it.

    Nothing ever jumped off at the spot either. That's what those other cats were for. They handled the girls, and guarded Ragga and Tray. That's all they did. They never said shit. They were some raw niggas. They were niggas that Ragga, and Tray grew up with but they didn't work the blocks. They were recruited and hand picked by their fathers as he had associates. But, you couldn't expect them to do ordinary things like most children and have the everyday type friends. They were on a whole different level. They did different things with different crews growing up because their people had their own things going on. This was sort of 'the sons' of Ragga and Tray,s father,s bodyguard type shit. They began to feel their own way in life. These brothas stood at doors, opened doors, and watched shit always. That's it.

<u>Me Tears</u>

We called them, 'Them Niggas' on the street. They didn't speak to anyone on the block. Under the Stab, they would give the pits and rotties love. They were one in the same. They had the same job as dogs, they bit muthafuckas. I know damn well I wouldn't ever pet them dogs, but them niggas feared nothing. They had the low down on the entire business, and was attached to nothing or no one but the business. We didn't even understand their involvement. Maybe they just liked to hurt niggas. The way they carried themselves was as if they saw right through you.

Me Tears

Them Niggas

When Them Niggas came around that meant nothing was going to happen. The problem was, something probably had already occurred, or was about to occur. Seeing them was the most peaceful time on the scene. When Them Niggas showed up, that meant Ragga, Tray, Queen, or Steph was around. Even if you didn't see one of the four, you knew they were in the 'hood close by. Them Niggas knew everyone in the crew, every crew family, and shit like that.

Once, a crew family member got popped. He wanted revenge, but Tray wasn't having any of that. Tray said that it would make things too hot on the block, and that the police would think that it was a 'street thing'. The fact of the matter was, the brotha was owing some other nigga for some shit, and hitt'in off a piece of ass that wasn't his. Anyhow, the police caught the brotha responsible about a month or so later.

The brotha was being held at central

booking with all of those other cases waiting for arraignment and stuff. His problem was he got caught on a Friday. Anyone who has ever been hit up for some shit on a Friday knows how far away Monday seems. Well, Tray found out and we knew nothing about it before hand. One of Them Niggas ran a red light on Saturday, they say it just happened that way.

They say that he had no identification, nor any registration for the car. When he got locked up, the next thing on the news Sunday was that nigga who popped one of our crew member people. He was found dead in the cell or something. They say he died of a heart attack or something like that. No one knows what happened. But we knew Them Niggas did that shit. We didn't "know-know", but one plus one equals two. The same one that ran the light got out of the lock up that same week on minor shit. Now that's how you beat a murder rap. Not that he murdered the cat.

They didn't live around us. They lived in next towns and places like that. I think that the only people knowing where they lived was Queen and Steph along with Tray and Ragga of course. It was a myth that

<u>Me Tears</u>

they had wives and children. They did the 'hood -like thing from nine to five. Sometimes you didn't see them for weeks. At other times we would see them on a regular. It was better seeing Them Niggas than not.

    Not once did I see any of them with any of the women of the Queen's, and Steph,s stable. The worst and probably the most scariest thing, or should I say perplexing, was to see the respect they showed to the older women and men of the area, not to mention the children.

    No one that wasn't apart of the streets got hated on. We couldn't and didn't deal with people who weren't inside our world. They saw to it. It was like breaking the law to do otherwise, and relate to non-crew brothas. You could be putting your self in danger by being viewed as a loose end, and loose ends got cut, cut off.

<u>Me Tears</u>

Coming In - Blee

    Being chosen is some rough shit. Most are taken from the crowd of wanna be gangstas that hang around us from time to time. You have to be nominated by a crew member first. It's informal, and usually happens while niggas is almost out of their mind puff'in. Then, you have to "Come In".
    This is why you have to watch what you say around the way. Niggas take shit for serious. One brotha wanted to be in the crew so damn bad he did the unthinkable. He and a home-boy, relative of his decided to open up shop on a corner two blocks away from our joint. I knew the nigga, it was Blee. Ain't had shit against the brotha. He was mad cool with the crew and all. But, that shit, that's what death is made of.
    He was a week into his little shit when it happened. They said he was in the back watching his partner work the block they tried to start. He had the heat. He had his Mac, and some other heat. But, he couldn't hold it down.

Me Tears

Some niggas went with one of them 6 to 6 niggas, and blazed the spot. They caught one of them, but the nigga with the heat wasn't your everyday type nigga. He trooped for real. Even though his boy was on the ground crying and shit, all hit the fuck up. That crazy nigga started hopping fences on the backside of the spot and caught up close enough to them cats in the car to spray the car and took out a tire or two. They say them crew cats went hauling ass down the street and made it back to our block about a half minute later.

Now, that was some fucked up shit to even come back on the block. Not to mention they didn't kill that nigga. To add injury to the insult of it all, the nigga knew them now. What was funny at the time, is the way those crew members began to pop up from everywhere. They were coming across fences and everything. But, when it was found out that they didn't do what they were suppose to, shit got ugly. Then, they started to make the muthafucka they were suppose to 'did', sound like a damn super hero or some shit.

"Yo, Yo man we crept on them niggas with the lights off and everything man. We just popped the lock to this old ass ride across

Me Tears

town and all." Some of us knew better than to listen to the crap. In no way would one of us slip up and say "Them Niggas" in the same phrase with this situation. At first, we thought they popped one of "Them Niggas"- "Them Niggas".

"Yep, Yep" one of the other flunkies co-signed. His ass, and all of their ass were up shit creek anyway. We just didn't know they didn't get the nigga at the time. We gave the failures our undivided attention. We probably should have gotten first dibbs on busting a cap in their ass.

"Then yo, yo, T-Black started ripping them muthafuckas, hanging out from the top of the roof on the passenger side and shit," one continued.

"Shit yeah nigga. You seen that shit?" Black co-signs.

"Then we got the fuck out nigga. Shit, that nigga was laid the fuck out dawg."

"Then, this....this nigga came from no fucking where man, bucking."

"Well what the fuck y'all hot ass doing 'round this bitch?" one of the crew said.

"Yeah, Shit Yeah.....Y'all done fucked up-up," another said.

"Shit Yeah, big time," another said

Me Tears

"Damn."

"Yo' man, that cat was running at our shit like he was the fucking law man."

"Well, y'all niggas know who the law is. I ain't saying shit. Don't put me in this shit. Don't even tell nobody you told me about this shit," another member said.

"Word," we all agreed. Those of us having no part in the fuck up.

They didn't know that same brotha had sense enough to run back to his spot. He got back to his boy before the police and shit. He stripped his boy clean and said they were walking home and some niggas sprayed them. We knew that he said that because the police was one of ours, and that's what the Stab knew the next day. That is the only reason shit didn't get to that point. I knew, because I was the muthafucka who had to go and check out what actually happened. He said he didn't see who sprayed them, which was good. But, he knew.

Ragga and Tray had gotten wind of what had happened and had some plans of their own. They were gonna take the nigga out the old fashioned way. But, first things first. That 6 to 6 nigga and them

Me Tears

other cats got missing real quick. Not one person knows how it happened. It felt like Them Niggas. You couldn't say that shit. The favorite line spoken every other sentence was: "Yo, where them cats at? You see them?" We were all working like walking around on eggshells, and pins and needles type shit.

"I don't know man. Um' just doing me," most of us spitted. We didn't want to know shit, and it was no time to come even close to short on a bundle neither. I was sure everyone else felt what I felt.

Blee, the nigga that shot at 6 to 6 was gonna be next, and I knew that. I couldn't speak on it. Me and him were still cool. I hadn't seen him in a while until I saw him that night telling the police that they were walking home. I didn't even know about the drive-by. I was just following orders. My job was to get the nigga out of the house he was held up in.

He was next to the projects with his grandmother. The shit wasn't personal, I just had to bait him out, and that's why people get shot at for real. Someone told someone that this bringing Blee into the crew was my idea. But, no one knows the nigga who said he heard me say the shit.

<u>Me Tears</u>

"It's been said." That type "He said," shit is what gets a nigga busted on. Worst of all, it put me out front and seen. That shit ain't peace at all, that being seen shit. Now, I know what the fuck a roach feels like when you turn the kitchen light on. This shit wasn't going to be nice at all.

"Yo' man, we straight?" I raised my voice from the sidewalk in front of his crib. I could tell he had some heat on him. At best he was peeping out the door because it was cold outside to him.

"We cool nigga," his eyes shifting back and forth, up and down the street.

"How ya' boy?"

"He straight. He be in for a minute. But, he cool."

"Yo' man, that nigga wasn't 'pose to do no shit like that Blee. I was try'in to bring you in man."

"Yeah," he looked right, then left spitting over the rail.

"Yo' man, that shit wasn't smart posting up a spot like that."

"What the fuck nigga, I don't eat, I die any muthafuckin' way. I'm good. Shit happens. I'm just not try'in to have it happen to me."

"Word......Still Wanna Yo?"

<u>Me Tears</u>

"What?"
"In."
"Yo', go 'head man."
"Nawh for real-for real. I wouldn't be posting up like this man," all I could do was look up at him.
"Hold up!" He put his head in and the door closed, opening a minute later with a nigga standing in the door with a jacket and hoody on. We sat on the step leading up to the porch at the gate. It was the right thing to do. So, I twisted up a spliff.
"Nawh, can't light that shit right here man."
"Take a walk."
As soon as the nigga got across the street, shit broke out. Niggas came from across fences on his ass and everywhere. Two dogs were under the street light on the corner a half of a block away. I knew it was a Stab. They were beating his ass – like 'for real'.
"Yo', get off him," It wasn't convincing at all. I didn't even try to help. I recognized right away that those were my niggas. I ran back to the porch.
"Call the police," I shouted to his grandmother, as people were watching

<u>Me Tears</u>

from windows and porches. Blee was holding on to the fence. Niggas were trying to drag his ass.

"Call the muthafuckin' police?" I heard coming out of the house. His grandmother, dressed in a long, blue, with yellow flower night gown, and rollers in her hair with glasses started her own music. POW!!!POW!!!!

"Get off my baby," another Pow!!!!! Doors on porches started to slam, and lights went off, as brothas had ideas of hauling ass. Looking at Blee, he began to swell at the jaw and the left eye. But, he wasn't stressing.

"U'm alright ma."
"Yo, I ain't........."
"Shut the fuck up."
"All I know is that I was told to let you know to be at the spot tomorrow at 2:30. This ass kicking was none of my idea dawg. I just thought I'd smoke one with you. That's all dawg. But hey, take this." I handed him a bag and a cigar. His grandmother went back into the house to use the phone and put away her shit before the police came. We could hear them.

"Where you going?"

Me Tears

"Come now dawg. I ain't got shit to do. If you weren't in by now, you would be dead by now."

"Word—"

He came along with his seventies limp. That didn't stop him from pulling on the joint or keeping up. He didn't say much of anything. Him coming down the street scared me. I know good and well my ass wouldn't be coming down the street after all the shooting and ass beating. Blee just had something in him that most didn't. When we made it to the corner where my ride was, I noticed one of our own. I knew that because of the dog. It caught my eye first as he was sitting, and his boss was on my hood. That's some shit Stab would do just to let you know. If it was any lesser brotha, his ass would have been popped.

"Damn, what happened to this nigga?" It didn't help Blee, and then again, he could have cared less. That was a true putting salt on a wound type shit, because he couldn't yet see Blee. Secondly, how would he know something was wrong with the nigga.

"Niggas man, you know..." I answered.

"Shit, better to be niggas, than Them

<u>Me Tears</u>

Niggas."

"Word."

"You that nigga right?" Looking at Blee. Blee wasn't giving a fuck about him either.

"He that nigga?" Trying to save face, looking at me. I knew, he knew, he was that nigga. He just had to have an answer. Shit, Blee wasn't feeling as if he owed anyone shit. He only wanted to mellow on the smoke. He, that Stab nigga, needed to talk to some niggas that had answers for his ass.

"Yeah Big Brother," I nodded.
He snapped his fingers and the pit got up along with the rottie lying in the grass. Jumping off the hood, he stepped to Blee and gave him some love.

"Yo, put that shit away. I got the shit." Blee still didn't say shit. He simply nodded his head, and got in my car. The dogs and Stab got in the back.

"Don't worry about these babies, they trained." Big brother handed him a couple of sacks and a few sheets, and cigars.

"This shit for your tomorrow pain cousin."

"Bless," he got a word from Blee.

"Yo, here man," he handed Blee a few

<u>Me Tears</u>

bills.

"I'm straight."

"Boss said get you something to wear."

"I told you."

"What you told?" Stab said.

"If he wasn't gonna be down, he would be down under by now."

"Now, that's word."

"Yo' man, get some gear. I'll be at you at about noon—word."

"Don't listen to this muthafucka. He don't know if he's gonna make it through tonight." We all nodded, and not one of us said a word. It's true, you never know.

"This the nigga you want to see," pointing at his own chest. "Now, Them Niggas, you don't want to see them."

"Word," I said. Blee was looking around from window to window like a brotha was about to get popped.

"Don't worry dawg. You won't see Them Niggas, and if you do. It's probably too damn late," as I laughed. "Word."

That's how things usually happened. Niggas get missing. Brothas pop up. People are added, and subtracted. You never know. One thing was for sure. Blee's recount of that night was far more

<u>Me Tears</u>

believable than them other shit heads. In either case it was too damn late for a couple of them. The ones that Blee put caps in. The ones in the hospital.

Blee thought they were left for dead when he went back for his cousin. That's when that elf looking nigga came to work. They say he tightens up loose ends and shit. He was the 'laughing' in your face kind of guy, but you couldn't laugh with him because it wasn't sincere. It was more or less one of those 'if you fuck up, I am gonna get you, can't wait to get you' laughs. It made me nervous. People that don't give a fuck about their teeth like him and treated women like he did, they have no heart at all. He was a nervous cat. He was Worthy's cousin.

Worthy, he and Tray go way back. Worthy lost his mother to dope. She did the street thing, got the chicken and that was that. Worthy, he never knew his pops and was all his little cousin had. Worthy was both mom and dad . Worthy hid him from the system, and reform several times. Dre, that's his name, never went to school and only knew how to count money, and hurt people. A true hoodlum.

So, when them popped niggas went to

<u>Me Tears</u>

the hospital and the police had all that shit to sort out. It was Dre who went in and took care of them. They said he paid someone who worked there a few 'things' for a hospital uniform for cleaning or some shit like that. It didn't matter how he did it. They got popped while lying in the hospital getting treatment. Even the brotha that didn't get popped by Blee, we didn't see him for a minute. The strength was in the survival, and not in that almost shit.`

<u>Me Tears</u>

The Barber Shop

    It wasn't long before we began to make our own presence known on the block. Blee had begun to take shit to a whole new level. It was Saturday, right after hustling all night. We did the ususal shit that most crew did. Friday night was a peaceful night, no one got shot or shot at. You would think it was safe. But, there we were at ten in the morning trying to get our shit done. We had left a couple of broads at their apartment. We met them a few weeks back at the spot. They came by a few more times and walked our spot on the block, copping weed. They invited us over, and since they had their own crib, we did.
    We stepped up at about half past six. All the dough was checked in with our Six at about half past five. Of course we didn't have any heat, not heat-heat, just a piece to keep a nigga off our ass while we hauled ass. If need be.
    Bev was the darker skinned chick's name. She was ugly as o-get out, but the

Me Tears

ass was banging. To a brother like Blee, it didn't matter, and who gave a damn anyway. She had a gold tooth for real. It was off center like it was suppose to be, with a nose joint, and mad holes in the ears. She didn't have any of her things on the finger. The pajamas tried to hide that ass as she walked in front of us from the door. Even though she was feeling Blee, the nigga wasn't stressing my checking her out. From 'go', I knew he was going for his. Sheila was in the bed asleep.

"She-She," she yelled.
Now Sheila, she was as fly as the next queen. Same chocolate complexion but natural. None of the extensions or shit like Bev.

"Go on in the room," Bev said.
"Yeah, go the fuck in the room nigga," Blee's eyes got big, as he took a seat, and began to roll one up. We didn't have one all night.

This was our first stop. We didn't know if we would hit them skins or not. But, we knew about getting smoked. I had the forties. Them shits was cracked before Bev said a word. I pulled the covers from Sheila after putting shit down

<u>Me Tears</u>

on the table. She was not impressed.
"What the fuck man...Yo! Quit with the bullshit," she said rolling over not opening her eyes.
"Hey baby," I whispered.
"Who the fuck let you up in here?"
"Bev! Didn't I tell your ass?" Stopping mid sentence, as she focused.
"You said stop by."
"Damn man, I just crashed," she got out of bed and went to the door of the bedroom. I followed as she went into the bathroom. Blee was trying to finish the dutch. But Bev was on the job, just that quick.
"Damn," I smiled and reached for the smoke.
"Gimme the shit man. You'll never get shit done like that......Damn," looking at Bev's half shown ass.
   Blee reached for the bag from his pocket, Bev paid me no mind.
"Look at that bitch," Sheila said.
"Wanna Smoke?" turning around.
"Smoke?" sounding surprised.
"Yeah, smoke," I was surprised.
She shook her head and rolled her eyes, going back into the bedroom.

<u>Me Tears</u>

It wasn't long before I finished a couple of joints. I lit one and passed it to Blee. Then, reaching down I began to rub on Bev's ass, and her legs separated a little for me. She started to moan as I rubbed up between her thighs as she gave more space to me. She was slurping and popping Blee like today was it.

"Mafucka, this is the life," Blee exhaled, as I began to rise a bit and lit the other one.

"I be back," walking back into the bedroom. Sheila was wide awoke with some cartoons.

"Why the fuck you niggas come up in here at this time? Damn."

"Look, I don't need this shit. I'm out."

"I'm just sayin'," as I passed the joint.

"Shit, we wanted to get busy. But hey, if your girl down, and you ain't, we cool." I knew Blee didn't mind my joining the party out there.

"Move over," I sat on the bed and kicked off my shoes.

"Nigga you sick," she started to laugh.

"What?"

"Stop playing."

"What? What? You ain't w'it this?"

"You must got me confused."

Me Tears

"Move the fuck over...shit."

"Don't talk to me like that. You ain't my muthafuck'in man nigga."

"Look Sheila, I ain't got time fo' this bullshit. Keep it real."

"I can't today. That's all."

"Damn, It had to be."

"Well hell, that's real as you can get."

"You know what to do. Work with a nigga."

"What?"

"Will you move the fuck over. Come on now. Shit, I'm tired as fuck."

It wasn't long before she came around, for real. She slid under the cover, not wanting me to see and all. But, that was cool, it worked. I could hear my dawg in the other room making much noise. I was wanting to be out there. I had felt up on Bev, and she was definitely a better situation.

"Hold up, I got to go to the bathroom," as I rolled out of the room. Blee was squirming like a baby, Ooooing an aaahhing like a bitch. I went towards the bathroom and circled to where Bev and Blee was. By now she had turned, but her PJ's were still up. That wasn't a problem as I reached to

<u>Me Tears</u>

pull them down and she stopped me. It didn't take but a second effort. She lifted one leg and slid it out of the pajamas. She had the smoothest, blackest ass I ever saw. I was more than impressed. She wasn't rusty and grey, but ain't nothing wrong with that either. I picked up a hat from the table and slapped it on as she was to the side a bit, ass in the air.

She was warm and wet, red like fire, ass big, yet firm. Not that I was critiquing it, and no sooner than my starting , she was working me back as well as Blee. We simply gave each other the fist, as I saw Sheila leaning against the wall, with her arms folded.

"Whatever," she turned and walked away, back into the bedroom. Blee started to laugh and give me some more dap. Bev didn't stop, and I began to ram in and out until it was over for me. Then, she hatted Blee and straddled him turning around and pulling me to her. She removed the hat and began working me like she did Blee. We stayed a minute and then I had to go and get my shoes. As I got to the door, I noticed she had locked me out.

"Yo! Can I get my shoes Sheila?"

"Why you try to play me?"

<u>Me Tears</u>

"What?"
　"Whateva."
"Can I get my shit? Shit, you said I wasn't your man. Just let it be that then........ Damn. Shit, you got condoms all over the place up in here. Be for real."
　"Them shits is Bev."
"Right, you don't use these shits," the door finally opened.
　"Fuck you," she went to the bathroom.
"That shit don't matter."
　"These shits is hers," she came back into the room, and threw one at me.
"Well, I'm borrowing it." She sat on the bed.
　"Keep them shits."
"Come on let's just do this."
　"You sick nigga, I still got a day or so."
"Take that shit out or whateva."
　"What?"
"Go in the bathroom and handle your shit, damn."
　"Get the fuck out of here."
"For real."
　"You better go see Bev."
"I don't want that trick, come on."
　"You just fucked my girl and you .....You

Me Tears

sick nigga."
"Hey, I thought shit...I thought shit was like that."
 "Now you know."
"Exactly, I know. Come on. Tomorrow?"
 "Tomorrow?"
"Yeah, I come back on my day off Monday then?"
 "What the fuck that gotta do with shit?"
"We can go to the movies or something."
 "What movies or something?"
"To the mall or some shit like that."
 "You got amnesia or something? Nigga you just had your dick in my girl."
"Yo, I ain't doing that shit no more, word. Just you, not her," she looked at me.
"Just you, damn. I didn't know how shit was. How the hell am I 'pose to know shit like that? Damn, if she knew you was fill'in me like that, "Why the fuck she let me do some shit like that?" Surprised.
 "That Bitch knew."
"Well why the fuck you pissed at me. I sure as hell ain't know shit. Now, I know...Damn."
 "Y'all nigga don't give a fuck."
"Hey we going out?"

<u>Me Tears</u>

"I don't know."

"I bet that nigga ain't going to no damn movie with Bev....that's word. Here, take this and go get something to wear aiight? I'll come through on Monday. Just keep it if you want. Just let me know so I don't have to walk all the way the fuck up here."

"Stop w'if the bullshit."

"Hey, I see you at about three. You could be my broad Sheila."

"You ain't got one?"

"Not fo' r'il, you know what I'm saying? Shit, you chicks be getting that ninja dick and shit, you just probably cool 'bout that shit."

"Yo, I ain't them bitches you be fucking with."

"So what you saying?"

"Let me know what's what."

"Them bitches don't get no lips here honey."

"Kiss me then."

"Hell nawh, I don't know you like that yet."

"What wi-fee mean to you then?"

"Don't mean no kissing and posting a nigga up and shit."

"When a nigga get married the nigga kiss

<u>Me Tears</u>

his wife.....Wi-fee nigga."
"Yo! Let's roll nigga," Blee shouted, and the both of us got up and stepped into the livingroom.
 "Yo! bitch, don't be fucking my man no more. You knew what time it was."
"Yeah Bev. Why the fuck....?" I added.
"You let that nigga gas you Sheila?" Blee was in the doorway behind Sheila.
"Yo, we heading to the movies Monday. Y'all down?"
"What nigga? Please, I ain't got no time for no shit like that pimp."
 "Fuck it. I'll come," Sheila injected.
"Shit nawh bitch. this 'bout me and my nigga."
 "I can't go?" Bev looked at me.
"Nawh, this is us yo."
 "You sick Dawg," Blee laughed.
"Let's bounce. I gotta get my shit done the fuck up. I ain't got no time for this 'Little House On The Prairie' type shit. Shit, let's roll."
"Word."
"Monday," she said. I didn't look back as I stepped.
"Yep."

Me Tears

"Monday," Bev said.
 "Yo, check your bitch son." I laughed at Blee.
"Whatever trick," Blee laughed, as we bounced and headed to the Hill.
   The pizza house wasn't opened yet. It was only nine by now. He was up inside the joint getting ready. I had the number as I stood in the door pressing the numbers, and then I could here his phone ring.
 "Pizza House," he answered.
"Yeah, let me get a large extra cheese, with mushroom."
"Sorry, we not open now."
 "Look at the door."
"Oh, hey," he laughed.
 "Yo, get my shit ready, and don't burn the crust this time," we laughed. I grew up on these pizzas.
"I be back at nine thirty."
 "No, no my friend. The oven not hot yet. Takes time, takes time."
"Ten, not ten zero one, you know what that means?"
"Okay, sure. You strange man." as we laughed.

Me Tears

I had to go across the street. Blee was already in the shop. It was crowded like any Saturday morning. We waited, taking in the usual barbershop bullshit. Niggas crying about everything under the sun, and not forgetting to over exaggerate the amount of Friday night pussy they got, or let get away. Three kids were in the chairs getting their hair done, as the mother of one of them was outside smoking a cig. The other two were from around our way. They were the next generation of us. The type that would say: "Fuck you," in a second.

Down the line were a couple of cross town niggas. They usually got cuts to keep from the shit on their side of town. We could tell they had a long night like us, but we got paper for real. We didn't hate them cats, but this was our spot even though they grew up in our section.

The young rats were enjoying the conversation, which we tapered when the lady came back in the house. We kept shit light. She was hot. The type woman who's life would be spoil if she got up with niggas like us. But, at the same time she looked as if she could use our thug in her life. It took like what seemed forever to

Me Tears

cut those little monsters hair. I decided to stop outside to get a paper. The door to the Pizza house was open. I grabbed the papers. I paid fifty cents but I took a couple and gave it to my pizza guy for extra cheese. He knew I had jacked the machine, but he was going to sell those papers I put on the counter.
"Where you get the papers my friend?"
 "From my friend, my friend."
"Oh, I see," as we laughed.
 "Hey, don't forget the extra, you know."
"Hey, hey, when you didn't get the special pizza?"
   It wasn't long before I had my breakfast in my hand and headed back across the street. The boys were in the chair, and the mother and her son had almost finished. Clearance, and Bo had gotten into two of the chairs as I sat down and started to grub on my first slice. Blee didn't say a word. He was focused on getting his 'fresh one'. No sooner had the door closed behind the lady and her son, the shit had started it seemed.
 "I got that son," Blee told one nigga.
"What?" The brotha was there first too.
 "Tell that nigga. That's me." Henry just

Me Tears

closed his eyes.
"Yo' man, please not today fellas."
"I ain't trying to hear that shit man. Word son."
"Who you the fuck son'in?"
"Yo, this me dawg." As I bit my first bite of my second slice.
"You don't know me nigga." I was trying not to laugh as Blee was getting serious. I knew he was going to do some crazy shit.
"Yo! Come on! Chill." Henry pleaded.
"Yo!, you want a beer nigga?" Blee looked at me.
"Whateva man," I answered.
"Get the fuck up and get me and my dawg a couple Heinies nigga."
"Nigga what?"
"This my shit man."
SMACK!!!!!!!! Blee hit the nigga.
"Go get the fuckin' beer nigga."
"You must be outta your fuckin' mind."
"Yo!, please Bell. I mean, Blee," Henry said.
I loved watching this shit, but I wasn't going to let my pizza get cold. I hated cold pizza. The cat tried to reach as he turned. CRACK!!!!! Blee hit him with a right, and he

Me Tears

staggered. My heat was already out. I could see the brotha was packing from the bulge to his side. I passed Blee the heater, and he grabbed it as if he said 'gun', like a surgeon says suction. It was right there for him. The people started to get out of chairs by now and move. No one left the shop. Henry looked away.

"What nigga?" Blee asked. The cat didn't say a word. He was pulling but nothing happened. I was waiting for the niggas brain to be all over the place. Brothas were saying "no man," and "Don't." Blee looked at me. I hunched my shoulder.

"Nawh man, we got shit to do," Blee smacked him with the heater. The other brother took the bat and started to swing at Blee backing up and out of the door. I could tell there was no getting our shit cut that day. I wasn't sitting in that mutha, not after that. The other nigga let off a few punk ass shots as he ran through the alley, drawing heat. Only moments later, police came. I had passed the heat to one of my 'round the way niggas sitting across from the package store at the square. Blee had gone running the fuck down the street, jumping the tracks. No sooner than you could wink, a cop came running my way.

Me Tears

"Around there," I pointed, eating a piece of my pizza with the box open.{Stupid Bastard}.

About thirty minutes later my dawg brought my shit to my crib, and I gave my man some weed, and we smoked one. "What the fuck happened?" We laughed, looking at each other.

"I don't know man."

I had to come up with better shit to do on Saturday mornings. I began to love Blee for his attitude. Later, he explained that he just wanted to get some sleep, and that the brotha was crazy. The one thing about it is, Blee didn't adjust well to discomfort. He spoke like the brotha knew he was working all night or something. It wasn't long before we squashed that minor matter. The Stab went to the spot those cats held down across town and settled the issue. They handled shit like that. Queen came around to let Blee know that shit wasn't cool like that. She had one of the barbers come and hook Blee up ever so often after that incident. They would go into one of the apartments and handle shit.

The Stab and Tray respected that type shit. Blee wasn't that smart, school wise.

Me Tears

But, he had to have a certain order. When it came to gear and grooming, he didn't play. I even heard him tell a chick that he would slap her if she dropped his own cum on his pants. He thought professionals don't do shit like drop cum and shit. Now that, I could understand.

"Don't get none of that shit on me bitch, I will smack your ass." He moaned.

Me Tears

Queen and Steph

They both came up in the Benz. That's Steph's shit, Queen sported a red Benz. Same shit, only different colors. They both had on this mini skirt and high shoes type things looking like twins. They each had their hair in rap with native African jewelry, and D-ray was in trouble. They began to whisper some shit to his ass. He looked at one and then to the other , and then across to me. I was mad as a brotha could get. I was wishing it was me across the street, but thanking the Almighty I wasn't. Them chicks were trouble.

He shook his head in the negative, and then Steph looked over at me. I signed to my nigga watching me and he hopped the fence, as Queen pulled D in the alley. I was hot but my shit was on the curb, and I was clean. But Raz had to see what the fuck was up with D. He was working and there wasn't any time for shit like this.

I sat on the porch, looking at Steph a minute and she didn't pay me any attention. Or, so I thought. She was just in the shadow of the tree next to the porch where D had his shit. Then, she turned and bent over touching her sandals like they needed to be laced or something. I couldn't be seeing this shit. The boss would kill me sho' nough for this type shit. Her skirt came up over her cheeks, and I could actually see a bright yellow. She was wearing a thong but I was focusing in on ass cheeks. She had a big ass. Like bees to honey I scooted across the street.

   "What up Steph?"
"What up w'it you?" she smiled.
   "Not a thing."
"What you want?"
   "Nothing, didn't you call me?   What's up w'it Queen and you tonight?"
"I thought your job was sitting across the street and watching shit, not worrying about what the fuck up with Queen and Steph."
   "Right, peace." I got up and started back to my spot across the street. A couple of custies came up and Steph served them. She knew where the shit was. That's the cool thing . She worked the spot before, before we even became a crew. Even before The Establishment, her and Queen

Me Tears

and Them, like boss and Ragga and the Stab, during the days they weren't supposed to be out here.

    Between custies, she came over and rubbed me up a bit. Then, as I stood to the side of the porch after one of her sales, over by where my heater was. She came over and backed up on me. We slid further to the back of the house out of sight. I could only feel her ass against me.
"Say you want me," she teased me.
    "Shit no. I ain't stupid."
"Say It."
    "Hell no, I don't want you BabyGirl." We were at the corner of the house by the back porch now. No one was working. I pushed her forward to the porch and pushed her shoulders forward unzipping my pants.
    "Say it."
"Hell no," I said as I found my spot with her. I never called her BabyGirl before. But, I heard Ragga or Tray say it once or twice. Leaning back a bit looking down the alley. I kept my balance by grabbing each side of her ass and digging in and clawing her to me.
    "How can I want some ass that ain't

Me Tears

mine? This time it's me, next time who the fuck knows?"

"Why you gotta say that." She moaned.
"You know?"

"Know what?"

"Cut the shit out," as I backed out of her and turned her around looking towards the street, pushing her head down. It wouldn't go.

"You must be sick nigga."
"Oh, it's like that?"

"Nigga please," sucking her teeth.
"Fuck it then Steph," as I turned her back around and continued.

"What happened to BabyGirl?"
"Nigga please." That's what the fuck happened.

It would not had happened if we were on the ends of the spot. Tonight we had the middle. We only had the powder. People that wanted us, was usually people with dough. They couldn't get shit by car. They had to walk down. The base was on the end, with the base. Shit switched up everyday. I began to think that one way streets were made for the crews that slang. The weed niggas always had the bikes. It was impossible for us to get

Me Tears

bumped off like I heard other crews did. There were just too many of us. I couldn't spend no more than a few minutes with Steph. Even though cats knew we were okay, they would circle the area with those bikes.

    We had the beat up pick up truck parked on the street as well. It didn't belong to anyone, and we could role it out anytime we got ready. Shit, we even had the spike pads like the police. We could roll them out and flat niggas tires if need be. There was no catching us at night, almost. We were very aggressive in maintaining our block at night. Only the police had dibbs, and some of them were on our payroll. I was hoping "G" was alright.

    Queen was said to be with both men and women, after her and Cuz first broke up. She liked getting eat out people said. She even did the threesome thing, they say. They say she was rough at times. One nigga was said to have gotten a cracked jaw when she hit him for no reason with brass knuckles because he wouldn't get on his knees.

    Then, after they wired his shit back and he came back to work. She came back

Me Tears

to the block and gave him a job, and started talking some crazy shit and apologizing to his dick. That's what niggas say. He saw the whole shit from across the fence. That's what Raz said. Then, she bit the nigga shit because he told one of The Establishment who broke his jaw. She didn't bite his shit off, or anything. But, he sure did learn a new trick on his knees when his jaw healed.

"When your shit heals, you gonna do what the fuck I say, you understand?" The nigga had to understand, 'cause she had her shit to his dome, and threatened to pull the trigger. Sure thing, as soon as the wires came out his mouth. Queen came back around and sat on the porch, and spread her legs one night. She had on a mini that night.

"So, what you gonna do nigga?" The brotha didn't say shit, he crawled up the steps to the porch and buried his face. Then I knew just how crazed she was.

"I brought you to the side of the house before, because I liked you. Now look what you made me do." She moaned with her head back, petting his head.

"But, that shit wasn't good enough for you. You had to let shit be known, and

Me Tears

shit. I know you liked me too. You just didn't know how to say shit baby." I couldn't believe I was hearing and seeing this shit.

"You want the world to know how much you love me, and I love you more for this shit. You know how to love me daddy. Hell yeah," as she gave Steph the thumbs up. Steph, she was in the car, not believing this shit neither. I knew she was one sick bitch from that night on. Then, she asked the nigga some out of the world shit.

"You wanna lick my ass out here or you want to go to the side?' He didn't say shit. Queen got up and started towards the back. He followed her out of view. I didn't say shit. I only looked at Steph rubbing in between her legs, sitting in the car. Then she looked at me. That's the first night I was with Steph. Those quick things did not count.

"What's up?" She said looking at me.
"What up w'it you?"

I made it to her and leaned over into the car.

"Nothing just waiting for my girl?" As she reached and grabbed me, stroking me

Me Tears

a bit.

"Yo, I ain't like that nigga. You crack my jaw or some shit. One going in your ass for real."

"One going in me?"
"Damn Right"
"This one, how about this one right here. Come here," as she got my attention.
"Nawh, fuck that. Ain't got time for that shit. Yo, get Queen and tell her that nigga gotta be working now. It's Friday. Niggas got paper and it's the first of the month. She's fucking up shit right now. This shit ain't correct. Do this shit some other time...man."
"Oh, I see. You running shit."
"Hell nawh, that nigga needs to be on point. Shit is heavy tonight. You ain't sucking my dick. You don't get no attention......not tonight."

"How 'bout tomorrow?"

"Sunday or Monday."
"You see me Sunday or Monday?"

"Shit, I ain't fucking with you Steph."
"You will if I say so."

"You try that Queen shit if you want aiight?"

Me Tears

Blee and JBlack

I was with this nig from the start. Don't fuck with a man on a rainy night all geek the fuck up. You'd think that shit would go without saying, at least until I bought my first car. He said he was straight. Blee was in the back and I was just trying to be cool with JB. The nigga just got out of the hospital. I didn't know what the fuck was going on at first when I threw him the keys. Blee was hittin' on the joint and passing it to me.
 "Let's Go," Blee said as he started laughing. JB hit the gas and started to turn around the corner, then to the other block always turning left .
 "Shit yeah," Blee said, as JB started to shift up and down as he went left after left.
 "Yo man, What's up dawg?" Looking back at Blee.
 " What?"
 "This muthafucka ain't from around here or some shit?"
 "What?"
 "What? We just went around this bitch

three or four damn times," as JB kept shifting gears.

"Hurry nigga, punch that shit, they almost got our ass, damn nigga!" Blee shouted. JB got serious, and started to speed up looking in the rearview mirror. The left and then the right mirror. I started looking around.

"What? What?" Looking at JB, then Blee. "I got this muthafucka!!!" JB said, gritting his teeth, and looking around.

"Yo man!" ain't nobody back there. Slow the fuck down nigga 'fore you total my shit."

"They coming nigga, damn."

Then all of a sudden the car stopped; it was raining very lightly out. JB started looking around.

"Where the fuck they at J–, Where they went dawg?" JB's eyes were as big a plates. He got out of the car and dropped to his knees looking under shit.

"We straight," JB said then he pulled out a bill and took a hit of some powder and he passed the shit to me.

"Nawh nigga, I'm straight," as I put my hand up.

"Oh shit, Damn," the car jetted as he got

Me Tears

up off the clutch.

"They—,Oh, shit J, come on nigga, they got us."

"Yeah, muthafucka, yeah, Mario damn it, I got this shit Blee."
"What the fuck nigga," looking back at Blee was no comfort to me, the brotha was laughing.

"Yo!! Pull my shit the fuck over nigga. Give me my shit back," Blee started to laugh harder. He burned up damn near a quarter tank going around the same damn block. Then suddenly, the nigga hit the brakes, as I turned off the ignition. Just as quick, as the car came to a stop, JB opened his door and went running down the street in the rain, as the headlights caught him. Blee was laughing so hard he was crying tears in the back seat.

"Would you look at this shit?" JB was waving us on in his direction.
"Run," he shouted, looking crazed. As I turned around, all I could see behind me was Blee's teeth, and him holding his gut.

"Look at my nigga, look at that nigga," he laughed, winding down the rear passenger window.

"Run nigga run. Oh shit, look at my

Me Tears

nigga."

"What the fuck is wrong with your cousin nigga?"

"You on fire JB," Blee shouted as we followed JB around the corner.

"Watch this, check this," Blee started to go crazy, slapping the headrest.

"Your shirt's on fire nigga," Blee shouted and JB started to get undress. I started to laugh. I couldn't believe this shit. The nigga was running down the street butt naked a few seconds later in front of the headlights.

"What the fuck up with this nigga Blee?"
"Wet, dust-man."
"What?"

"Nigga hit some wet and shit earlier, now the nigga hitting that powder. He'll be aiight, just chill. Let me get that muthafuckas clothes and shit.

"How the fuck you gonna stop his ass?"
"You don't. Stop what?"
"Look at that nigga."

"Shit, that nigga free. Nigga, that's the most down brotha I know. He ain't scared of shit but whatever the fuck be chasing him when he get high the fuck up. Other than that, the nigga straight—word."

Me Tears

"Word dawg, but look at this shit man." Blee busted out into laughter again"
"Yo J, Yo Jay!!!! I got them muthafuckas man," Blee yelled at JB.

JB looked back and his pace slowed down just as quick.

"Word Blee?" Butt naked and all the nigga was looking around as if he was checking for someone to clear shit.

"Yo! He got all them muthafuckas dawg," I added, not knowing what the hell I was saying. I just wanted the shit to stop.

"You straight, we straight." Blee smiled.

"Yo man-Your shit man, put your shit on man. Them is leather seats man."
"Chill, chill," Blee said.

"Yo Chill? Nigga you chill. The nigga ain't got no damn clothes on and I know he don't be wiping his ass. If he don't give a fuck about no shit like that, you know he don't wipe his ass."

"Yo J man, here man," Blee pasted him a blunt. There was no more handing that nigga my keys.

Me Tears

BLEE MEETS SIX TO SIX

It was Monday, cold as fuck too. We didn't need a dime. We went to the 3 spot. Everyone was paid, and that didn't matter the least. Blee was with me and JB his nigga from around his way. JB was the brother of his cousin who had got popped. JB was brought in not too long ago. The Stab and Ragga decided to let them in. The only condition being, they worked different spots, and shifts. Mondays and Sundays were the only times they were together. They had their own peace when we were out. They grew up together, like brothers. We were sipping before we got to the spot. JB had his forty and Blee had his half pint and we passed both and the blunt.

It didn't matter that we stepped into the club like that. It was not like most clubs. This place had lights, lit up like Las Vegas, real leather chairs and real carpet, and shined, well kept, hardwood floors. There were no VIP section or anything. Tray and Ragga didn't do shit like that. The crew knew to move. We all knew the best spots, the corners and side tables where the booths were. If a Stab, or Them Niggas, Queen or Steph rolled in the joint, you got the fuck up and squatted somewhere else. No one waited on anyone, except for when The Four, Them Niggas and The Stab popped up. Their shit was always walking to the table before they got seated. The new cats in the crew had to always repeat themselves. The older cats simply walked to the bar. The trick in getting the best service was to drink the same drink each night. Otherwise, they would ask you, "What you need?"

"That....that's that nigga that heated me," Blee told JB after we sat down. It was that 6 to 6 nigga. We thought he was did by Them Niggas.

"What?"

"That's that nigga-word." JB never met the nigga before. This was only his second time in the joint. JB didn't act like much, and didn't say a word as his dimenor got relaxed and he became distant to our converstion. "What y'all want?" JB asked, standing up

"Just get whateva dawg," Blee puffed on the blunt, exhaling.

"Word," I added. JB went to the bar and put the forty on the counter and said some shit to the bartender, that six to six cat. Then, as the brother reached in the cooler................. CRACK! JB smashed the nigga, and jumped across the bar on his ass. Then, the nigga came flying over the bar, and JB was right behind him. Not a second into this shit, he smashed the dudes head into the table.

Not one person reached. We were family. Everyone knew what the matter was. Blee was still puffin', knowing this shit was going to happen, laughing. The chicks giving dances backed up. Brothers were not even upset. Niggas were collecting. Blee was stacking. Not one person ran out the joint. "Get that nigga," Blee laughed. Twenties started to hit the table as that six to six tried to do a little something. JB started to stump the brotha. "Muthafucka," that's all JB could say with each kick. Then a chair, and then a kick. Then, nothing as the door swung open. It was Tray and one of his fly chicks.

The music stopped playing for the first time. Tray didn't say shit as brothas started to move. Them niggas was admiring the beat down, looking at crew as they moved out the seats. That cat was still on the floor getting his senses about him. Tray didn't say shit. Both of us started to try and help clean the mess up. Tray knew what it was about, and ignored the entire moment. His drinks came to the table as usual. Some cats in the crew helped that beat down nigga from the floor, and into the back. Queen and Steph came in moments later seeing the mess.

Everyone knew it was JB. The nigga was still amp, huffing and puffing, and puffing on smoke a bit, as we straightened the table and picked up the broken chair.

"What the fuck happened?" It was Queen in some four inch heels, and legs as long as California, looking down.
"Ask them muthafuckas," Blee said.
"You being smart?"
"Nawh Queen."
"Yo! What's this?" she looked at me.
"Some shit Queen. Niggas, you know."
"Why the fuck you breathing so damn hard nigga?" looking at JB. One of them niggas was over her right shoulder assessing the situation.
"That's that nigga."
"What nigga?" looking around, arching

her eyebrows.

"Back there," pointing.

Queen stepped to the back door, and in came Steph.

"What the fuck happened to that nigga?" Steph smiled. When she looked at JB, Queen saw who Steph was talking about, looking over her shoulder at JB. They started to laugh.

Tray didn't say shit one way or the other as Steph stepped to JB.

"Y'all some trooping niggas," she took out some heat and put it to JB's chin. JB didn't say anything. He was still upset with not beating that nigga some more.

"Tray want your ass," one of Them Niggas said to JB. Blee stepped with him as Steph patted Blee on the ass.

"Leave my man alone," Queen smiled. Blee was her piece. Steph had simply smiled. That's how it worked.

"Sit," Tray said as everyone looked, and Steph sat on JB's lap. Tray ignored Steph sitting on his lap, kissing him and wiping the sweat from his forehead. JB was only 5 feet 9 inches or so, but could hold his own with the best of them.

"You too," Queen pushed Blee to the

ME TEARS

table.

"Y'all niggas f'il me," Ragga came in the club with the "What the fuck going on" expression, pulling his glasses. Some of the members started to whisper at him before he got to the table. Queen sat on Blee's lap and put her arms around him, kissing him to the cheek. The fellas sitting down started to finish cleaning up the mess, as one of Them Niggas bought in Tech. That's the name of the nigga JB waxed. Ragga took a seat at the same time his drink arrived.

"Why are my sisters ass on your laps?" Neither smiled or said shit. Both looked at Tray. The ladies leaned their head on each of their shoulders, stroking their chest.

"This shit is squashed. F'il me?" You got a problem w'it this nigga?" Looking at Blee.

"That wasn't it."

"That nigga popped my peeps. Let a nigga pop your ass," JB snapped.

"Chill, Chill baby," Steph said.

"Gimme some heat. I'll smoke this bitch right now." JB looked at Tech.

"Word," Blee said.

"Be nice baby," Queen urged Blee.

"You want this?" Tray looked at Tech. "This is the type shit that happens when niggas fuck up," Ragga laughed.

"Now that nigga got the right idea," Ragga pointed at JB.

"Y'all listen the fuck up," Tray took a sip. "This shit is done. He ain't sorry he popped your boy," as Tray looked at Blee. "Y'all niggas should have both been pushing up daisies. That's my fault for giving this nigga the job in the first place. That's my peoples, sorry as he is."

"Word," Ragga looked away in pain, catching Raz as he came through the door. "What the fuck up peoples, my niggas?" He sat next to Ragga, whispering.

"So, they meet," Raz said as the Stab was in the house. Shit wasn't a secret. Raz was the other 6 to 6. Although he was a 6 to 6, he was just another brother who could get it. The only person working at the moment were the newer cats in the parking lot, keeping eyes out, and Them Niggas. Any time was their time.

"Yo! This shit over. Give that nigga some love. Sorry, he ain't dead your ass like I said. Do you want in this shit?

ME TEARS

'Cause we can't be fighting ourselves. You can't drop out and don't worry. I'll send his ass back at your ass. He miss again, y'all niggas both six feet under-word. Y'alls in or what?"

"I'm in."

"Word," said JB.

"What the fuck you want?" Blee looked at that nigga.

"Fuck it. I'm good."

"You speak on this shit ever nigga, it's on for real nigga. I'll heat yo' ass word," JB looked at Tech.

"Any y'all niggas got beef?" JB looked at Raz.

"Betta get the fuck outta hear nigga."

"Y'all niggas want a fair one bring that shit outside wheneva nigga," Blee said.

"Yo, do your job nigga and get me a drink," JB told Tech.

"Word," Tray smiled.

"'nough that shit. Y'all get the fuck from 'round here. We got shit to do."

"Damn Blee. Say some more of that shit. I think something in my heart moved. You know?" Queen said.

"Can you get the hell up off me so I can

get the fuck out?" Blee grilled Queen who slid onto his lap during the conversation. Ragga started to laugh.

"Get this nigga something to drink. He don't want no pussy, before I let him bitch smack your ass," Ragga looked at Tech. "Bitch ass Tech," Tray laughed.

JB and Blee left the table leaving the four to converse a bit. Tray had his girl to go with JB to calm him down a bit. "You fuck him bitch, and that be your last," Steph meant it. But, things were different, Tray gave the okay.

Victory was her name. She sat with us that night, and a few of her friends joined us later that night. We all left together, and crashed at one of their apartments. That sort of relaxed JB a bit. Steph was really wanting me however. She did blow up the cell an hour later and the next thing we knew, both her and Queen were at the apartment. Both of us, me and Blee hauled ass on JB.

Just for the road, I quietly slid up behind one of them chicks and went for mine again. I covered her mouth at first as not to stardle her and handled my business. Walking out the door, I was realizing that

ME JEARS

this was a once in a lifetime moment. I couldn't believe it, looking back over my shoulder, shaking my head.

JB got stuck with the other three, something I couldn't handle as I had lips and feet all over me before the call. I didn't know that certain body parts had such feelings. From my toes to my neck, I was attended to. Then, they began to pull out all sorts of tools and toys. JB said he hit shit up most of the night that night.

Kingstree, South Carolina

"Yo dawg, have a sit", Tray said pulling on a 'L'. He just looked at Raz.
Exhaling, "What the fuck now?"
"D-Wak and Youth got down last night." he said.
"What the fuck----Where?" Tray's eyes went from relaxed to serious as it could be.
"South Carolina man."

"D-Wak said Youth called your moms and said they needed Justice."

"That's peace," Tray relaxed.

"Nigga's was smok'in and shit," Raz continued.

"Weed charge?"

"Yeah."

"Not the 'caine nigga?"

"Just smoke, 'bout an o-z or some shit like that."

"Bagged up or loose?"

"Loose."

"Get on that shit. It's Dwak shit nigga. Got dreads right? That's the move. He got priors?"

"Nawh- It's Raw."

"Word then, Y'all roll down that bitch----Now. Take Taneka, Cal-Slim, Viv, and Ragga will back y'all up. Take those niggas off the street, all that shit. Give them troops a vacation. Tell Ragga to hit them muthafuckas off with five a piece until shit comes home. Meet up at the stable. (The stable was the basement at the building, that's where we set shit for the block).

The same way we were taught the ropes and went from place to place to cop our blow. Them brothas had the old route. The Florida connection that Dez passed down to Ragga and Tray. Even though they knew the cats better and shit was straight with those people. Sometimes things get too comfortable, and niggas relax. It was like an every month thing to them.

There were no excuses for not showing. Everyone would be up in the house except Tray. That nigga didn't play no shit like that. Besides, he and Rag was very seldom seen if ever in that spot together. That was hot. Ragga knew what to do. Given this latest, they could have been watched, set up or something. This was no cell phone type conversation type thing. It was law, that Ragga spat for Tray. The only relaxing thing about seeing Ragga, was that you didn't see him by your damn-self. That's word, peoples got ghost around that brotha, and no one knew what happened. They would just say a nigga got 'Rawga'. It wasn't 'Them Nigga' type shit either. The worst thing is, when brothas came back to the block if that was the case. They would have broke ribs, leg, jaw, arm, and all manner of shit caused by Them Niggas. Ragga, he was the justice arm of this operation. Sometimes, brothas would be found broke the fuck up out of town like they were kidnapped. They would come to work and say: "Yo' man I was kidnapped." You just knew that it was Ragga, or Them Niggas. When the money didn't come back straight, usually that's when your ass got late, that's when your ass would be brought inside. But, when you were safely broke up like some cats, you would hear niggas say: "Thank God."

You didn't know what they did wrong, but they knew. Maybe when he was breaking them up, he told them. I asked a couple of them, and they would just say: "I don't know."

Ragga was Tray's right hand man. He didn't trust anyone else. Tray was said to be a Raw brother himself. That's what they would say to each other when they worked the block. It's like us saying 'peace', or 'one'. Them brotha's, even the ones on lock, said Raw. They were the only ones saying shit like that. They didn't use no signs or handshakes.

Seeing Ragga, and hearing him speak was spellbinding. He didn't waste not one word. "You understand," is what he said after each statement. We knew better than to ask him to clear shit up, like we didn't understand. Pain was not seeing the brotha at a meeting. Those were minor meetings. After the minor meetings we would have on a weekly bases, crew members would get busted up. Once in a while when we came out, one of 'Them Niggas' would be outside. Niggas would start sweating and asking: "What?" Saying: "What up?" Knowing they wasn't gonna answer. Some cats just started to bitch out, and trying to make deals. Some would start blurting: "I ain't do nothing."

    He didn't say much when he came up in the joint. The bullshit haulted. Niggas just looked. He was black as all hell. His dreads were flawless. The grill was priceless. When I say 'flawless', I don't mean pretty. They looked animal, like lion type flawless, strong. The nigga had his original shits. He still lived at home. You never went up to his mom's crib, not for shit. "Tray sent me," had better been the first name coming from your mouth if you rolled up on him spit'in anything. That had better be followed by "Got Shot"-word. No doubt, he was the money man.

    "Check that shit in," he started as the crew began emptying pockets. This was no time to act quiet either. Bundles, dough, and all kinds of shit was hitting the table, mad condoms.

"Stand the fuck up," his brows came almost together as he flossed his diamond and platinum grills. Tray had the same shit, saying the same thing–"Rawga". Niggas moved like they racing in the Olympics not to be last standing.
"Take all my shit off, and place that shit on my shit," he looked at Queen. Everyone started unsnapping shit and putting it on top of the stack in front of them. We knew 'his shit' was the dough. We didn't have shit. Watches, chains, everything, even grills came out. Everyone knew not to floss your grill in front of him either. We all started to look human, and felt naked. I mean, some brothas weren't seen since grade school. Everyone knew which heat belonged to which crew member.

    From the bundle to the bling, all the shit was the crew's shit. It was all Tray's shit. If you did something exceptional, you were given some bling type shit as an award. A brotha couldn't wear no shit to work, not like that. On your day off you could, but why? He dressed us well. On our day on the brick, that was some other

ME TEARS

shit. You couldn't swap shit either.

Tray did shit just so everyone knew. Everyone's style changed at different times, depending on what your job was that day. One thing for sure, on your day off, you didn't go around working niggas and vice-versa. You didn't bring no chicks around working niggas. Chicks around the crew, was the crew chicks, and that was bond.

{Days off went in pairs and threes. On days brothas was off you still had your heat. But, them shits was clean. At work, them shits was yours, meaning hot just without bodies. Tray didn't go for that type game, stupid shit. It was better to ditch some shit than be caught with it, product or heat. The steel we had on our days off was always
someone else's heat. It could be mother or father shit, or yours if you didn't have a record. The tune was always the same: "Shit was stolen"

Ragga had a suit case, 'Them Niggas' brought it in. He never carried shit. Big Steph and Queen had bags. The shit was in order as niggas knew not to say shit to Big Steph or Queen. Those were Ragga and Tray sisters, 'nough said. Them chicks fucked you when they got ready. If they didn't like your ass, you could come up short. That's why some cats didn't know why they got broke-the -fuck up, I bet. They didn't have a man, neither of them. That is, until they said a nigga in the crew was their man. That meant that they was gonna throw some ass your way. You didn't have a choice, and was no need arguing the point. Just as fast as you became their man, you could be not their man. No questions. They were some fine sistahs too. The nails were always did, hair tight always. The shit they sported was shit no one ever seen before on the block. I mean, they could come on the block to pick up and go shopping. Niggas couldn't say shit neither. You couldn't say shit to Tray or Rag neither. That shit could get you killed, and when they wanted a piece, that was that. You couldn't tell a soul. You didn't know who was tapping what. Spice and Bun, Trays cousins were the only ones I ever heard called either of them 'bitch'. Nigga's knew not to say shit like that. They collected too. But when they collected they dropped off. When them chicks collected, muthafuckas tried to get ghost before they saw you.

ME TEARS

Usually, shit would happen with them, by them just letting Tray and Rag know they needed something. Sometimes they would send one of us to Victoria's or something for women shit. That was it. You went. You had no ideas 'bout nothing.

Once, I was just being lookout. It was a mellow Thursday. It was the middle of the month, and shit was peace. Niggas was broke and we didn't do credit. The Establishment did credit, not us. Anyhow, I'm just lounging on the porch across from niggas working and here comes big Steph and Queen. Queen didn't say a word. She carried a shine-.380. I knew because the shit was at my nose, and Steph had her hands in my pockets.

"This for You," Queen said as she put her pink, gold encased cell to my ear.

"Yo boss," I knew it was him on the phone.

"Ya'll close that shit down." Steph had her hand massaging my crotch, directly in front of me.

"Word?"

"You can't hear nigga," he snapped. "You and Zulu go w'it Queen," the phone clicked.

I gave them brothas across the street the signal and they spread the fuck out. Zulu was my soldier. His job was to watch me watch them. He packed more heat than hell. He never touched shit, not money, not shit. Being early evening I knew we were doing some chick shit. Ragga didn't like the women going about outside the 'hood without members. So, I guess this was the day they chose to let them off. Steph didn't put my rolls back in my pocket . I was only holding about two grand at the time. Shit was slow, and that was the snatch from Tuesday. From the vile to the tree, everyone knew what was what. The blue was the tree money, and the red, the base. It was no problem with the trees or the red. 'Cause the crew didn't do red, and trees was for off niggas.

If the next day was your day off, it was duty to cop a couple of sacks. If a member came up short on a tree bag or two, we knew he was crazy or wasn't working the next day. There was no need to cop on your job day neither. Shit was free. You also got paid on that day too. So, if you checked in and the females came before you checked in. You were caught out. You had to see Ragga or Tray 'cause the

ME TEARS

captain, or whomever wasn't hearing shit.

You had to find Tray or Ragga and just stand there looking stupid. You never rolled up on them talking. That shit pissed them the fuck off. They were gonna be pissed off any way if the sisters jacked you. The worst part is, they didn't tell you one way or the other. Brothers holding would always ask: "You working right?" The sisters would always answer the same: "Shut the fuck up punk." Or, they would say some ole other shit niggas didn't want to hear.

One day, this nigga 'Sting' had to go to the boss after Queen saw his ass. He was the first cat to call Queen 'bitch', other than Spice, and his cousin. He didn't know. "That bitch snatched my shit," is what he said. When word got around to the brothas in the crew, we were trippin', the dude couldn't find a friend, especially when he got called in.

This was some up front type crap. He made it out of the shit, but to hear him tell it was worth the price of admission. He said the boss, Tray, looked at him with Queen right there. "My sistah a bitch?" he asked. All he could say was: "I- I-I-I." Just thinking about it, that was a great choice of words.

"I-I, what nigga? Let that be the last. Your ass gonna be hang'in with Queen and Steph the next couple. I hope you got some knee pads muthafucka, 'cause you probably gonna be eat'n a whole lot of pussy. I just hope shit ain't bleeding or noth'in like that. That's some nasty shit anyway. But, bleeding—get the fuck out," Tray said. Sting said the shit wasn't bleeding though. That's all he had. They wouldn't give him no pussy. They would just come on the block and bring him around the back for about a week or so with some chick that had an account. They always had on dresses and skirts. Sting took pride in that shit for some reason. He said life was better. I don't know what he meant by that. It was just better.}

We all knew something was up. Queen put a bag on each crew member shit, and Big Steph held a bag and each member put their own shit in the bag. Queen started from the other end. The Establishment knew what was going on. I could only imagine they were here before. But, for the most of us, we had no idea. Ragga had his shades from his eyes, and opened the case.

One by one he started to stack . The shit was crazy, he had twenties and tens coming out of his ass. I saw shit go into his bag, but never out. You would think someone hit the lotto. There were twenty of us in the crew and another twenty in the Establishment. We sat back to the table. Them Niggas had the wall along with the pits and rotties. I thought we did well and were getting bonuses or some type shit.

The sistahs came back around with a duffle bag and collected all of the smaller bags this time. No one touched the bags, but them. If you ever touched one of those loot bags, you were done. They said it was like taking a steak out of Ragga's mouth. That bag was put to the left of Ragga as niggas was trying to figure what the hell was going on. Then Queen began picking up the stacks and putting them in front of each of us. This was a good thing. Ain't no need giving a nigga a stack if you gonna dead his ass. When we all had a stack, Ragga started to speak.

"Y'all niggas is on vacation. Go see your peoples, bitches or whatever the fuck. Don't be on no block. Y'all get the fuck outta sight.....word. Stay the fuck outta sight until your cell blow the fuck up. I see your ass, I dead your ass...word," Steph got up and put cells on our stacks along with a beeper.

"Don't let them shits ring and some bitch pick up my shits either. That beeper beeps, you call the shit on the beeper from a pay phone with the calling card. You use these phones, I got something for your ass...word. Nigga's don't be on no fuckin' phone. Don't take none of them cats you been fuckin' with, with your ass either. Plenty pussy in the world. {Then Queen started to pass out some bus tickets}

"I don't care where the fuck these tickets send your ass. You let them speak to you, and that's where the fuck you go. You go where it says, and you come back on the day it says, unless that damn phone rings otherwise. You don't tell your mama or nobody. You disappear...Poof , or I disappear your ass. If anyone didn't hear or understand what the fuck I said, say the shit now." He looked around.

"That be 10G each stack. Don't pack shit. Don't take shit. Just get the fuck on the bus. Two to a city. No steel, no nothing. Check your asses into a nice hotel, not one of them dumps neither. Not one of them palaces either. Stay in a different hotel each week. Don't be catching no cabs either, walk. Don't be carrying no bags, carry nothing. Do some shopping in the 'hood. Eat your ass full and relax. Now, get the fuck out."

That was it. Niggs just hauled ass after picking up the dough. The Establishment stood up and came to the table with their dogs. It was enough to bring a sweat to your ass each time one of them sniffed you.

{I saw a cat come up short and that nigga started to sweat and shit, and talk like he was crazy or some shit. Jam, one Stab, said: " hold him" and the pit sat down and the Rotti latched on to the nigggas pant, right at the belt zipper area. Ain't shit you can do, especially when the pit started to sniff the nigga. I saw the cat bitch the fuck out. The head of the pit started concentrating and moving up and and down like he was inspecting shit.
"Sit," Jam sad, and the Rotti let him go and sat.
"you too nigga," Jam said as the dogs were only a bit from a nigga's throat.

ME TEARS

"So, what the hell is going on?"

"I don't know. What is going on?" The brotha was trembling.

"You came up a bit light nigga."

"Light? What?"

"Yesterday, light." as he smiled.

"I wasn't light. I checked In."

"You had two bundles on Saturday and checked in two hundred not five."

"Yeah, but Queen came through and took a buck, and I had the rest. I was off, that left the rest."

"Queen seen you?"

"Yeah, Saturday, 'bout midnight."

"You ain't say shit?"

What the hell you want me to say man? What the fuck I'm gonna say to Queen?"

"Tru, Tru."

"Yo, Ragga was short on you,"

"Yo- man, that's my word. Niggas said that when Queen and Steph come, you check your shit....word."

"Word," the Stab nigga agreed. Other brothas even if they saw the shit wasn't gonna co-sign it.

"You know I can't snitch them to Tray or Ragga. I ain't 'pose to know nothing. I do

what I do."
"Word...Why the fuck you nervous then?"
"I'm wondering why the fuck I got to see you. I ain't do shit. Them muthafuckas ain't just decoration," looking at the dogs.
"Tru, nigga, you gonna be aiight."
"So, what now man?" Jam picked up his phone and started to talk on the phone. "Queen," he started.
"Nigga said he saw the Queen, and that shit ain't his business. Jam got up and started to walk away and the dogs got right the fuck up and followed him as they went around the corner, leaving cousin sitting there. I could tell the nigga was shook, but he didn't say nothing about shit. He posted and took care of business like nothing happened. Until the next night came. }

"You mafuckas, sit the fuck down back there. I'll be w'it you niggas in a minute," Ragga looked at me and Blee, pointing at the chairs The Stab was sitting in.

New Chapter

We were hungry, and still not knowing what the hell was going on. I guess by this being our first mission, things were new and we didn't know what to expect. So, we went along with everything. Ragga had me, Blee and a couple of other niggas I trusted to go to California and pick up some shit from Los Angeles. They had mad connections, and the show had to go on. We were a 'just in case' thing going on. Just in case shit didn't go well with that South Carolina thing.

As we sat at this Ponderosa, all of our nerves were at wits end. The ride from Cali was non-stop and niggas started to look, act and talk a bit more funky by now. Of course, we had to get a booth at the window. Not that we knew anyone in Milwaukee. We didn't have an enemy so to speak of in the city. We just didn't know how to relax. It beat the hell out of Blee and Raz taking turns arguing about shit neither had a clue about. Even worst, the ass holes began comparing fart, and burps.

ME TEARS

Raz was about to flip. He never been in a car so damn long.

"Damn, how much farther?" came from him every time we entered another city. What made it worst is the brotha had no idea how many states we had to go through, nor how big they were. Forget about explaining shit, I passed him the map and let him try to figure it out. It was the best thing I could of done. He kept saying shit like: "Damn, we way the fuck over here?" to Blee or whomever sat next to his ass. I thought they were gonna spray each other in the back seat for real. If I had a nickel for each time I heard: "You stupid mafucka." I wouldn't need this fucking job. When you have twenty bricks worth damn near a mil of them dead presidents, you can't sleep. Not to mention, Roy holding onto five and me holding onto another five in our bags, slung over our shoulders each time we went to the bathroom or something. The heat was always at the on, and food was only a detour.

If the police rolled up, we had to blaze, we had decided to go out smoking them shits. We had our senses about what had to get done. We planned this and decided

ME TEARS

to take our time. If it came to buckin'. We also decided that if shit got hot, not all of us would go down. The one not seen, would try to get away. We didn't want to lose all the way 'round.

Sitting at that table on the north-side of the city was in a way like being back east. It reminded me of the few times we squatted in Harlem. Shit, more Negroes than enough were on that side of town. MLK Jr. Boulevard is just like any ghetto U.S.A.. I was too tired from the ride thus far to enjoy a meal. I didn't want to stop but that was probably the only way I could get them to stop the bullshit in the back seat. They were about to kill each other. I would have let one of them drive, but they couldn't read the damn map.

This old cat was at the counter getting ready to order when we went inside at first. He had a stack of half off coupons. We were holding more dough than Pillsbury, but Blee had to work the cat for a coupon.

"Yo!" he said. The guy tried to ignore Blee. "Yo pops, what up w'if one d'em shits?'

The old dude wasn't dressed like he had much, he was just trying to get a meal at a discount. Looking up at Blee with his grey beard and dark complexion, and the red-brown wine drinkers eyes. His coat was worn and still he had a sense of pride in the way he looked at us. He looked as if he was going to get a dollar or two out of us, a cigarette or something.

"Yo chill man," I snapped. "We straight dawg" illin' Blee. The next brotha in line ordered. He was dressed like a pimp. He had on the big hat, pinky ring, and suit. A brotha dressed like that ain't going to work. It was obvious that we were in a safe place. It was just before noon. Either that, or he was reminiscing about days gone by. That may be me one day. I thought.

Even though the seats were there for take-outs, cousin went straight for a booth, and a booth by the window. I mean, I heard the man say take out. Right then, I knew shit was hot on this block, and we felt right at home.

"You peep that shit?"

"Shit yeah, ain't no need gettin' popped waiting on no damn spare ribs, or no sirloin rib tips fo' sho," Blee mumbled.

"Sirloin Tips nigga, ain't no damn sirloin

rib tips. What you think?" Looking at Raz.
"I ain't tryin' to think shit. We got 'nough shit to fuck'in worry 'bout." The nigga was right.
"You all can seat yourself," the young lady said with an attitude. I hated the way she talked. The ghetto poor hooch, with the faded micro-braids and fake type jewelry.

If it had not been for everyone that my eyes caught, I would have thought that she was only seating white people and that we weren't good enough to be escorted to our seat. But, there were no white people in the joint. She just had that attitude that made you want to get a piece of ass, but when you saw the mug, you knew better. Blee smiled at her and she sucked her teeth, as his eyes went from her eyes to her breast. She did have noticeable headlights. It was a break in the tension, but still, we didn't need the attention. The brotha before us that sat at the window, didn't even think about hitting up the buffet. You can tell he had shit on his mind. You could tell he was in the mix around this mutha' as well. Why would a brotha want to sit at a window on a rainy day. There wasn't a lot of chicks outside, and certainly not in this weather. It only made sense to sit in the booth next to him. He knew what was what, and if anything began to happen outside, he would know first. That said, I sensed that he knew we were into some shit as well. Just to let him know, I fixed a look back at him when he looked our way, just to let the brotha know that this shit was for him too, all day. Not even looking, real ghetto arrived.

    Yeah, we were definitely in the spot. Bertha came busting up in the joint. There is always a Bertha in every city U.S.A.. The chick was damn near purple, but she was people, standing there with her arms folded, hungry as five people. She had on the spandex and mini skirt combination. She had no business with Zebra stripes on. The jacket had no chance of ever being buttoned up. But, it matched with the skirt. I could hear her breathing all the way from our seats. Then, behind her came her sister. It just had to be, and I was being considerate. It could have been her mother. The expression on her face was of one not to fuck with. She just looked around constantly, with her eyes wishing it was her at a table eating. She didn't need all of that silver on her neck. She was looking like the poor female version of Mr.

ME TEARS

T. The smaller of the three had to be one of their daughter's, or a younger sister if one was a mother. She was just as wide, just not as tall. With her thumb in her mouth, she waddled from side to side, looking like she wanted the lunch bell to hurry up and ring. I was shocked that a thumb came out of her mouth, the way her elbow was moving up and down, she could have well nibbled the thumb off.

The bigger of the three, which was only a judgement call, paid the tab. The register closed and the smaller of them acted like she didn't know any of them, but knew where all the food was. The second one exhaled and wiped her forehead. It was either grease or sweat. I didn't want it to be sweat, it was only eleven in the morning it wasn't even hot yet. It couldn't have been rain, because they had umbrellas. Whatever the case, she was serious as if just suffering from an attack of sorts. We would had been ragging on her back home. Truth be told, she was a sight for sore eyes. It was time to eat.

Any other time this shit would have been humorous. The neighborhood crack head was present as well. To my left was a table of slingers. It was mid-day almost and they were just getting moving on the day. I could tell they were getting shit straight for the day and readying to take their posts on the block. We did the same thing back home. I could tell the lieutenants from the soldiers. No doubt, they were all strapped. They didn't give a damn about being gangsters right now. We were in Stella's and shit like that wasn't gonna happen up in this joint. It was more or less a living historic monument. Those dawgs were feeling the best part of their day. The eight of them had four tables, even though two would have sufficed. Not only which, they were spread out. Looking around, I could sure understand.

    I picked the Captain out of the crew. This was like watching a movie or something. He was sitting with his back to me. Dressed in a white T-shirt and head rag on, sporting a proper gold chain with a little shine on his wrist. He wasn't as broke looking as his crew. They weren't making real paper. Some cat about thirteen was sitting opposite him with a white head rag on and a fake diamond earring. He joked around too much to be in their crew, and he was to the window with a chick with a tattoo and hooch gear on, to his left.

They weren't stacking it though. Either that, or they didn't have the brains to spend it. She could have been his trick, 'cause our chicks back east, out dressed that chick on soldier level. Forget about Queen and Steph, it was no contest. Directly in front of him was her two bad-ass twin boys. I just knew they weren't his, and the thirteen year old wasn't his either, probably hers from the guy three guys ago. His phone was blowing the fuck up as he fielded the calls, and was probably making moves. Except for the call when I overheard him whisper some mack game, he was business. The hooch ignored it. Captain dude was just feeding the youth, and this chick. Winter was coming on and like they say in this city: "It's getting cold as fuck out, gotta find a bitch to lay up w'it."

Just as that was going on the crack head chick was served a porterhouse the size of Fred Flintstone's take-out ribs. But, she wanted them rapped, as she had a pile of plates emptied from the buffet. Her people across from her was doing a good deed by taking her out it looked. It was the middle of the month and her type only has money at the first. The hair was not did at all, not even tied up properly. The sneakers were dirty and the jacket was worn, very worn.

"Shit, I gotta get me some rolls up in this muthafucka, hell yeah, for shit later," she twisted out of the booth and back to the food cart. This could definitely be home as she came back with about four rolls.

"Excuse me sweetheart, do you think it would be possible for you to rap this with my entree?" she asked the waitress.

Now, I didn't have any problems with her style. But, I hate it when base heads start with the proper English shit. Just be indignant or be proper all the way. You would think she was a teacher if you didn't know any better. Then again, she could have been at one point. The couple sharing the table simply laughed.

"You betta not," the mother of the twins raised her voice. I caught the view of the twins as the guilty one was looking at her, and the other minding his business, looking at the brother. With his eyebrows arched, the brother looked into his other brother's face.

"Burrrrrrrrpppp," the guilty one let out.

ME TEARS

"You think I'm playing?" the mother said.

"Ha, Ha, Ha-------," laughed the brother, and the thirteen year old.

"It was hurting. It wasn't like I farted."

Then, "Blatttttttttt." The other brother let one out his ass. She had no control, as the Captain laughed while on the phone. He threw a napkin at the latter brother.

Bertha had made it to the oasis, and all reason appeared to have fled. Why not come back for more? I thought, as I saw the loaded down plate. She had everything on the cart, not to mention the gravy coming over the plate from the potatoes dripping from her thumb onto the floor. Ain't shit she could do either. The chick had another plate in the other hand as well. She was in it to win it. The four of us looked, and laughed at the things going on. It was a minor break in our day. The take-out guy eventually got up and left with his order. He went into a bar across the street. I felt better getting our food wrapped after we ate from the buffet a minute. You never know, the guy could have felt us like that, and had plans. Either way, we got ghost.

ME TEARS

Shit. Same

Yeah, I guess, this is the type shit you live for. We hadn't slept in about thirty-six hours. A nigga get paranoid as a muthafuck when you strap on some keys in Cali and have to haul ass back to the east coast. The only thing is, the brothas that say shit is 'cool' and shit, are the same brothas strapping on fifty years for real. That is the type nigga that get dissa-fuckin'-pear—word. F'il me? For me, I wanted a draw. I wanted my weed pipe. I wanted some of that sticky shit my man sent us back east with. It was proper, a brotha give you some traveling smoke after you pack a few keys on. Tray didn't like that type shit. We could have the smoke. He could care less about that. He just wanted his shit back, correct. If we fucked up his shit, somebody had better got dead, shot, lock-the-fuck up, or something. You could even get missing, just have the shit right. The last thing you want is Them Niggas looking for your ass. You fuck up big like this, you gonna try to get ghost, ain't no need trying to explain, or 'splain' shit.

I didn't need to smoke for my nerves or anything like that. I just wanted to test this shit out. I never had no shit like that before, the way it smelled and all. The only problem I had was keeping an eye on Blee. If he saw me smoke, the nigga would want to hit some powder or something and start hunting some tricks and shit like that. My cousin liked to hit the powder too. Between the two of them, we were protected. I knew, had I started to smoke, he would want his stash that I was holding. The brotha would have been sniffin' and some trick would have been smoking my shit while he got his dick sucked and all of us would have been caught the fuck out. That's how stupid shit goes down.

A quarter cake was his, outright, upon delivery when we got back. That was my word to the brother. Shit, he came along because of the other shit he does. 5-0 or not, he would put something in you. He wasn't a leg shot, or bust up in the air type nigga neither. He liked to give a brotha a head shot like Erika likes the 'rim shot' thing. The chest shot was only good enough to slow a nigga down. He would have no problem putting you out of your misery. For the sake of you being miserable, laying on the ground bleeding, he would pop you in the head. He didn't like the idea of someone he shot coming back on him. The last time he shot a nigga he didn't kill the muthfucka. But Blee, he did some extraordinary type shit.

"Yo, open your mouth," I remember him telling the brotha, while the dude pissed his pants, crying and shit. He got mad.
"Shut the fuck up, I ain't gonna kill you, and you ain't gonna tell nobody about this shit, 'cause if you do I'll make sure you dead next time. You wanna die nigga?" he asked. I hoped he didn't get stupid, he simply nodded. Then, he started to ask the man what he thought death was like.
"I don't know," he answered, as if he was going to have a breakdown.

"What you mean nigga? You right the fuck there. Death ain't but a second away from your ass. You right there, and your last breath is right-the-fuck there," as he pointed to a place that even I couldn't see, getting closer, and lowering his voice, attempting to entice an answer.

"You think I'm playing? What the fuck it

look like?" The brotha started to tremble, looking at the man holding the gun for a hint or clue for an answer to give. "Do you see light or dark? They say the shit is like a tunnel with light on the other side. You see the tunnel?" as he smacked the guy. "Don't fuck with me."

"I see the tunnel. Shit, I know he sees the tunnel and it ain't me you gonna pop." I tried to help.

"I can't see nothing but my babies man, please don't shoot, please," he begged. I wanted to stop him, but I never seen a brotha get smoked first hand to the head while watching. I didn't want to see the shit. I wasn't looking away neither.

"Oh, you think I'm playing," as he cocked the hammer.
"I see different colors, and water."

"Water? You see water? Yeah, Yeah," Blee said.
"......And green things that look like plants, but no ground." He repeated.

"What else? "Cause that ain't hell. Ain't no water in that bitch," Blee added.
"I see angels."

"You wanna be with them. Don't you? If I do you now, that means you will be

going to heaven," Blee smiled.
"No, no, please," he cried.
"See that's what I'm talkin' 'bout. Heaven be right the-fuck there, and niggas don't want that shit," Blee said, looking at me. The hammer came back to the un-cocked position.
"Get the fuck up. I sent a brotha or two to somewhere. I don't know where though. I just had to know. You straight dawg? You want to smoke?" the brotha shook his head in the 'no' for real.
"When you ready to go to heaven let me know. That might be the only good thing I ever do in life. That might get me into heaven too. Now, get the fuck out," Blee was serious, looking down. Usually, he would laugh. But, I could sense he was serious. Otherwise, he would have popped him. He never just 'popped' anyone. "You think he saw heaven?" Blee asked me a few minutes later after the guy ran down the street in his wet pants.
"I don't know man. They say people see angels and things when they drown or go into coma or something. I don't think you can scare a brother to see heaven. Shit, I would have told you I saw aliens if you

wanted to hear that too. Shit, muthafuckas ain't gonna want to get his fuck'n brains blown out." I felt relieved that he didn't pull the trigger. At the same time, if he went to the police and told about this shit. It would be me to really pop his ass. You never know at moments like that. Blee was the type to do it. He wasn't an 'oops' type brotha though, he would get you for real.

I remember what Blee told the brotha before he left. "We ain't gonna tell about none of this.......So........" looking at the cat. "So, I ain't gonna tell" he hesitantly answered Blee. That was the right answer.

Bang!!!! Blee let off a round. I didn't look at first. I didn't want to see the nigga's brains on the ground. Blee shot in the dirt. "Now, the next time I see you spittin' at any of them other side nigga's you gonna see heaven or hell. I really don't give a fuck," Blee said. Blee handed me the pistol after the cat got ghost. He was one of our new soldiers.

Then Blee didn't hesitate. He gave me the pistol. "Put this shit to my head. I want to see if the nigga saw heaven or was full of shit." He said.

ME TEARS

"Go 'head man."

"Yo, put the shit there nigga."

"Yo dawg."

"You my nigga right?"

"Chill man."

"Stop being a bitch."

"Right here?" Putting the barrel to his temple. "I see heaven. He was right. Pull it. Pull it man. I might not ever get a chance again to go man. Pull the bitch....Now."

POW!!!!!! It let off. He was still standing there. I started to laugh. The pissy brotha didn't know. Shit, I didn't know it was a starter pistol. But, you can't take a chance with shit like that. Sometimes he would bust off shots pointing right at niggas on the block. I understand now why he never hit one. He was a better shot than that. He would always say: "Next time." They would run when he said run too, not knowing he shot blanks at them, while he laughed.

"Mafucka, you were gonna do me? Me?"

"If that's what the fuck you want nigga."

"I should put my foot in your ass."

"Then I will pop your ass for me nigga. It won't be no fake shit either."

ME TEARS

"What?"

"I ain't fighting your ass. No fair one, or nothing. We either down together or nothing man. I ain't got time for the bullshit. We got enough shit to worry 'bout."

"True, True."

"Aiight then."

"But yo, why the fuck would a nigga not wanna go. Or, why would he say he saw shit that he didn't see? If I would have popped that nigga, he could have went to hell for lying man. I would have told The Lord that I was sending him to heaven. It wasn't my fault he lied. Heaven is good. Right?"

"You crazy as fuck."

The Promotion

We all got promoted so to speak, after the mission was complete and them cats got out of trouble in the south. I was brought in one day after Blee was to chill with me and learn the system. This went on for about a month. He only had to watch me watch the middle. Then at the same time he watched Raz, and how Raz watched me. He caught on very quick as to how shit worked from both sides of the block to the middle. Although he understood my thing, and caught on, The Stab posted him to Raz's spot one day and Raz was brought in by the Stab. They simply started walking down the street. Blee was healed from the beat down and was so smooth you never saw the nigga. He bounced around like a bug on the water and you knew he was always there. Their was no one better for the job than that nigga.

You learned not to ask questions when that type shit happens, then all of a sudden my cell rang. "See six to six." It sounded like Queen. Not a minute later one of the Stab came from around the corner and sat next to me.

"What the fuck you sitting here for nigga?"

I didn't spit shit. I hauled ass to the house. Raz was up in the crib with the other six to six. Those other cats was Them Niggas, I could see them in the kitchen with Queen. They must have come up from the back or something. I didn't see them come in.

"Listen the fuck up," Queen said with a half smile. "This nigga," pointing at Raz, "Is your nigga." You don't be just fucking with them other muthafuckas no more. This is your Six to Six now. This your ass now. Tuesday through Saturday, sun up to sun down nigga-word. See this nigga?" pointing at one of Them Niggas.

"You don't want this. This is some shit you don't need in your life. See them over there?" She was pointing at two puppies. "Them your shits now. They keep your ass company now when your ass get lonely. They go where you go. You see the Stab now. They see Them Niggas there." pointing at Them Niggas. Now, carry your ass on. You be your ass back here a week from today," she finished.

I got up, and no sooner than getting up, I reached for my dogs. I couldn't hear shit. The smile on my face was huge, as I felt in heaven.

"Yo Raz," I didn't have to say shit else. I just walked out the door. I ain't had to say shit else that nigga knew. I couldn't wait to get to the crib with my babies. Raz was with me every step of the way, begging to hold my babies. My right hand was Blee, I had to get him off the block, or closer to me. I didn't have anything against Raz, but Blee had the attitude I needed. Raz was their pick. I had my own. When you move up, you need all the help you can get. Besides, this Raz nigga, he was their boy. But that shit could wait a minute. I had to teach my dogs to grab a nigga like the other nigga's dog. I couldn't wait for them to take their first piece out of a nigga.

RAY-RAY

    The old crew was getting locked up by the one, two, five, and tens years. As the turnover increased on the block, the loyalty decreased. That happened before we got into the fray. Every year another one of those old dudes were coming home on parole. Tray and Ragga always respected them. First with gear, no car, and always with a pit and rotti. That's who them Stab cats be. They are the brothas from the earlier days. Tray didn't bless them with money or anything like that. He blessed them with respect and loyalty.
    Back in the day niggas like Boz, Love, and Snub and others went toe to toe for real with niggas. They say Snub got ten skins. They called him Snub because he liked to watch the old ganster movies and carried a snub nose .38. He got hit up for only one body. He had to cop to that just to keep Ragga on the street. They say they both would have gotten locked down. So, Snub took the one body, and got out after five. He's the type Stab nigga at the

top of the Stab. It's like he don't even work. Just his presence is enough, because everyone already knows.

    That nigga Ray-Ray or T-Ray whatever they call his ass got out not long ago. He was a true trooper. He saw one of the crew off post and just walked up to him from nowhere and smacked the nigga with a pipe.

"What the fuck wrong w'it you nigga?" I reached looking around at the crew on the block. But then, Raz reached on me. I thought I was on the wrong side of the team, planet, or some shit like a "Twilight Zone" moment was happening. But, without a word being said. I knew to stand down. Had I clicked on that nigga, whoever he was, I was through.

    When the Rotti growled, even Raz was laughing at this shit. He didn't have a look of concern, almost like he wanted to see two niggas get popped. Me for heating that nigga that smacked my boy, and anyone else just because. He knew the nigga, and was laughing from the smack down.

    "You gonna what nigga? You gonna what?"

Me Tears

"Yo- cousin," I said putting my steel away looking at Trump.

"This my cousin. Yo, this nigga right here is 'Happening' some call him. Y'all call him Ray-Ray."

"You... you... Ray Ray? What up son? Niggas be speaking out here on you." As I gave him some palm.

Raz and his stupid ass was still laughing trying to get a nigga killed. I couldn't believe the nigga. We weren't concerned about the smacked nigga. He was swollen, but we had doctors for that peaceful type shit.

"This shit ain't no fuck'in game nigga," Ray looked around. "My niggas laid down for this shit here," pointing at the concrete. "Y'all know how many of my niggas ain't here because of this shit we do nigga? Niggas out here bull-shitting. Who the fuck the Six. Somebody gotta answer for this shit. Yo- nigga," he looked at the cat he smacked with his now swollen jaw, and red eyes, shook. "Bring d'at ass over here bitch. My nigga Bean Head got smoked right the fuck there. You respect that shit. I got popped right next to that nigga that night, respect that shit nigga. Too Nice, my nigga, over there," as he pointed grabbing the nigga by the shirt and turning him. "Smooth," pointing another direction. "Wiz, Mac 109," still pointing. "You under-fucking-stand? Y'all niggas understand?" He looked around.

"Yeah," my smacked nigga said.

"This shit ain't no Nintendo muthafucka. You can't hit the restart button out this bitch 'cause yo' ass get caught sleeping and you want another bite at the apple. Just like that shit to your face can't be re-the-fuck-wound. You gonna hurt a minute for real nigga. You ain't on point niggas can cause muthafuckas to get dead nigga. Niggas see your ass bull-shitting, they think they can roll on your ass. Then, niggas got to get rolled on because of your nonsense. I catch you again, I roll on you all.....Heard?"

"Word" his brother said.

"You, now you did a little something. But, you ever reach on my ass again nigga........"

"Word!"

"Who got trees out here?"

"Raz."

"What the fuck you waiting for nigga?" Raz started to laugh.

Me Tears

"You wanna burn some?" Raz asked Ray.
"Raz, don't start fucking with me man."
"Here man, I gotta watch these niggas."
"Tru-dat. Y'alls ate yet?"
"Yeah."
"I was gonna say don't feed these bitches until they learn sump'n........word. I gotta go get my dick sucked."
"I got you cousin."

Ray and Raz went to the back, as Raz used his phone to call some trick for Ray. While Ray got his brain on, Raz came from the back. Pizza and Chinese food came about half an hour later. The block shut down for the rest of the Monday. Tray and Ragga popped up, and we all met at the club later that night. Ragga never showed up like this before, not for anyone. The entire Stab was in the house that night. Ray was a trooper.

Shit Changes More So

Steph had come back through on a slow night, and later met me at my crib. We weren't working that night, just holding down the block while niggas was getting product correct. They were at the house, cooking up shit. We were basically cracking forties and dutch all evening. Steph wasn't like Queen. She wanted a man. Queen wanted any man, and right now. She wasn't over the Cuz situation.

It wasn't a commitment type thing on my behalf. The business was going great and Bev and Sheila or Jaz and Flo, as they called themselves or as we called them brought some shit in the game. It wasn't her fault. She was from the block, a thug-like chick. A real ghetto-hooch. She was my lady. She could have been everyone's lady. She was fly as fuck but wouldn't let it go to anyone but me, I thought. I stayed with her on my off days. "Ain't nothing wrong with a little cut-cut," she would say. She didn't mind cutting someone.

The Steph shit was new and Sheila came by one night while I was on post to keep me company. Both were cool as could be. Bev wanted to give some ass to my man across the way. But, Queen had his head all fucked up. She told him she would bite his shit off. No matter how much I pushed the nigga to the pussy he wasn't having any of it. Even if Queen had multi-niggas.

So, Steph rolled up with Queen, who got out and sat with my partner across the way.

"You betta check them bitches fucking with your dick like that. Looks like they too damn close to me. See my man right here. This is how you need to have shit to be. Don't let me tell you how to handle yours. I'm just saying."

I didn't say shit. Didn't have to. Steph didn't say shit neither . Flo knew who Steph and Queen were. But, that shit didn't mean much. Flo didn't move one step away in either direction, neither did Jazman. I knew it would have been a good throw and Flo would have held her own, but beef ain't gonna happen at the money spot. Everyone knew that. But, from catching Steph's eyes, I knew I was more than a casual thing to her. Her entire whatever the fuck changed. She was different, but couldn't say shit.

"Yo, come here. Let me holla."

"Hey Steph," I got up.

"What up?" I knew what she meant.

"You know Flo and Jaz."

"Whateva, come here," as soon as I got to the car, Steph rubbed my chest. Flo was not cool with that shit at all.

"What the fuck is this shit?" Jaz looked at Flo with disbelief.

"Excuse you bitch," Steph said. Queen wasn't giving a damn. She reached and came off the porch.

"Is there some type problem with you bitches?"

"Y'all all get off the block," Raz said as he approached.

"Word," I joined. Shit was getting hot, and Queen would have lit both them. Shit would have been fucked up for a while.

I didn't have to worry about seeing Steph. What made it worst was that Queen and Steph did our schedule. No sooner had I had my next day off Steph rolled up to me and Flo at the Park. While we were splitting a forty and sparking up a few.

Steph and Queen came to the park with two cats I had never seen before. It was

Me Tears

cool and all. Everyone spoke, and shit was real. Jazman was getting closer to my dawg, cause she saw Queen with a man. I could tell my boy was hurt. He really liked Queen. Queen would just as well had been with the both of them. To let her tell it, he was still hers. Then both Jaz, and my dawg went to another side of the park to talk.

"I'll be right back," Queen said as she stepped in their direction. Flo came closer to me and began to rub up against me, and although Steph was with one, she was not having it one bit.

"Yo, come here." Queen shouted at my dawg who didn't say shit. He didn't much pay her any mind, as he and Jaz sat at a bench.

"I said come the fuck here nigga. Ain't you here me?" He just looked at her. Jaz looked from him to her.

"You think shit like that bitch?"

I couldn't tell who she was referencing with the bitch statement.

"What's up Queen?"

"What's up exactly."

"Nothing, just chill'n."

"Get down nigga."

"What?"
"You heard nigga."
" Go 'head Queen."
"You ain't feel'in me nig—? You don't know now?
"Yo, I ain't working. This my shit-word. This my time. Know what I'm saying?"
"This your bitch?"
"Bitch, I got your bitch trick," Jaz snapped.
"That's your nigga?" My dawg smiled. Shit just as suddenly became more live. Steph had smacked Flo with the forty across the shoulder and Flo clawed her weave. No sooner than that happened Queen grabbed Jaz by her weave and pulled her to the basketball court from the bench. I didn't know the niggas they brought to the park but the niggas was laying twenties and we got in on it. My shit was on Flo and Jaz. I mean, I would had bet on Queen and Steph but we weren't talking 'bout capping someone. It was our off day. Shit, Jaz and Flo been puttin' foot in niggas ass as well as bitches since I could remember.

When Jaz reached up and pulled Queen to the concrete and Flo ran away from Steph towards Jaz, I knew it was over.

Me Tears

Queen didn't see her coming as Flo ran in and kicked Queen right to the gut and Jaz jumped on top of her and began punching her like a man. The brothas knew those twenties were mine as soon as Steph made it to the court. Flo turned and they grabbed each other, and then Jaz got off of Queen who was pretty roughed up by now. Steph was covering up as the both of them swung on her like crazy.

    Queen got up and headed for her car, and my dawg grabbed Jaz, I took Flo, the other brotha took Steph's arm, she was swollen a bit. I picked up my dough and hopped the fence with my partner as Flo and Jaz hopped the fence as well. Now that, that was the bigger turn on, looking back at those two hop the fence behind us. Nothing like some down chicks like that.

    There was no need in staying around to get popped, not over shit like this. We slipped back to Flo's crib, the four of us. No one came out for two days, and no one came looking for us. As far as I was concerned, shit was over. My concerns didn't matter. Neither one of us were gonna speak on this shit. The Establishment would handle this shit anyway after they met with the Six to Six.

Me Tears

That's what they did. They sorted out shit. They were like middle management in the company. I knew how to handle this shit otherwise. But, I couldn't just let Queen and Steph know like I would some ordinary chick.

If we need anything, we went to them. If we had any problems at home you saw them. Niggas trying to fuck with you, they handled everything. That's all they did, handle shit. They were like the Justice System. We called them Justice.

The Establishment were the cats that opened up the block with Tray and Ragga when Dez left. They were their soldiers. They never came down. They took trips to unknown places. They mainly spoke to the captains, Six to Six and that's it. There were only two of them. The 6 to 6 day, and the 6 to 6 night. Then, there were the Off and On. They did the slow days that the 6 to 6 had off. They were like related to Them Niggas or something. They had no idea as to what was going on. They didn't care. Every time a crew member asked them On and Off cats something they said the same shit: "go 'head with that shit nigga, let your peoples handle that shit tomorrow."

Me Tears

They were like captains in training or something. They had the same type muscle as the Stab. But, you only saw them occasionally. They stayed on the block both days and never left for the two days they came.

Everything went through them on Sunday and Monday. There was no calling Ragga or Tray. It's like they were accountants or some shit. They counted and added, counted and subtracted. When Tuesday came, they left the words with the 6 to 6. They told the 6 to 6 of any problems or concerns and that was that. When things were figured out, last week was over. Not one thing was done about the incident at the park.

It was Tuesday of the following week and shit happened as usual. The dogs started to pop up. At first you would see one Stab and his two dogs, and then another and another. Dogs were circling the block, one block, then the next. Then, as soon as they appeared, they were gone. Later, a few would come back from the park and post the block. They usually let the dogs go at the park in the early part of the day to run around a bit. Shit, I felt the power myself. I had my dogs.

Blee

    He got bumped up as well. That nigga would do some crazy shit, for nothing. I learned to expect anything from his ass. He was like Elf, but with the crazy. Elf did a job and you could respect that. Blee, that brotha got into excitement. He didn't smoke before I met him and we should have left it that way.

    On one of our off nights, we were just sitting in the livingroom watching some shit on television, it was hot as hell outside. The windows were open and shit, and the nigga came diving through the window and everyone hit the floor. Muthafuckas were reaching, turned off the lights and the television and followed his ass in to the room on a low crawl. The nigga went under the bed. When I got there, he was breathing hard and panting, looking back at me.

    "Yo, yo. What up? I whispered.

"Them Nig, Niggas was after me."

    "Yeah, word? Them Niggas?' I asked. I knew we had a chance as long as we knew they were coming. Most problems came when you didn't know they were coming.

"Yeah, they coming for all our ass, all of us man." Blee whispered. I didn't think much of the shit. Elf was holding down shit in the livingroom and another nigga was at the back door.

"What's up?" Elf said, looking around to me.

"This nigga had some wet or some shit. Look at his eyes," Blee was sweating more than necessary.

"Mafucka," Elf said getting up coming towards me and Blee.

"Nawh, it's cool," as I held Elf back. Had he did some shit like that outside, Elf would have popped his ass. Inside, would have drawn too much attention, and have been too messy. We would have to explain shit to our peoples. It's anyone's blood outside. But, in your house, that shit is yours. The brotha spent the entire night under the bed.....watching.

Me Tears

Me and Steph's First Night

    Steph wasn't the bitch I thought she was. Being out like I was, you see some shit chicks do, and you learn not to trust shit. She didn't say much standing there with a half smile. With only a look as if she knew she caught me off guard, she gave me a smile. I could only lower my head and shake it from left to right. It was hard, not thinking about the beat down. I was pitiful, I wanted some. Very slowly, I was happy, a bit scared of this thing. She didn't drive, she was walking for some reason. Usually, an alley way or something did the trick.

"Where you going when you get off?" "You know. Where's Queen?" No sooner than I asked, she pulled up.

    One night after the first night that Blee and Queen was together she came to our spot, her keys dropped.{Bend over, Bend over}. She had on these fitting jeans and lifted from the waist when she bent. {Oh boy, what an ass..........Damn..}.

"You off in an hour or so tonight.....Right? " Steph asked. That meant I could get a flick in or something. She was jittery and that made me nervous. Why would she be nervous? I thought. "What the fuck going on Steph?" She only smiled, really smiled. One hour later, I called it a night and the fellas were packing it in. I went to the 6 to 6 and checked in. Coming outside, there she was in her car, parked. "Get in."
"Going to the movies or something? What's up with this?"

   I had never been to her real apartment. This was a long ride, about ten exits. When we got to the house, I was impressed. She gave me the keys and stood behind me and reached her arms about me.
"Are you hungry?"
  "Word!"
"Come on, let's get a pizza or something," as her hands stopped me from fumbling with the keys. The pizza house was just across the street. Her walking close to me when we got to the car let me know we were going to walk for it. I imagined that's what the hand holding thing was about. I wasn't use to this shit at all.

Me Tears

"What the fuck you doing trick?"
"Trick?"
"You know you want me Slim."
"Want what?"
"I know you do."
"You gonna give me some ass right? I ain't way the fuck out here for nothing. I got a perfectly good, ass kicking type chick waiting for me."
"Why you gotta........?" sucking her teeth.
"Yo, I just ain't got no time for no bullshit."
"You cut the bullshit." Mugging her forehead, she smiled.
"I ain't playing with your ass Slim," kicking me.

    We made it back to the house. We didn't eat at the restaurant. That would have been like some type of dating, holding hands type shit. I just wanted some. When we got inside, I went for the remote and sat my ass on the couch with the pizza. Steph disappeared around the corner. She went into the bathroom and came out later with this T-shirt on that didn't fit like it was suppose.
    When she came over to me and sat down, I could see those thighs as well as her hardened nipples. Of course, I had to

touch. But, she slapped my hands away.
"What is this?"
 "Gimme a slice."
"Let me kick my sneakers off."
 "Let you go in the bathroom Slim. I ran you some water."
"What you saying?"
 "Yo, you been working all day. Just carry your ass in the bathroom." I was confused in how to do this shit. It would have been over by now. I would have given a trick a thang, and that would have been that. Shit, I could go for two days and get my dick sucked at will for days.
   When I came out of the bathroom, the lights were off in the living room, and the television in her room was on. She had gotten under the covers.
 "You don't have to work tomorrow, so you can stay the night," she said.
"Stay the night?"
 "Steph, word. I just want some and a nigga is out."
"It ain't happening like that."
 "Why the fuck you bring me way the fuck over here then? I ain't got no time for this shit."
 "I know you use to them skanks and shit."

"Whateva Yo."
"I want you to be my man Slim."
"Steph, I ain't got no time for this type bullshit. I do business with your niggas, I ain't got no time to get into no shit with you. You could have asked me that shit on the block. You ain't have to bring me way the fuck out here for no shit like this."
"That ain't it."
"What then?"
"Nothing," her eyes were looking everywhere except at me standing naked at the bed.
"Why you acting like you never seen a dick before or something?"
"Don't play with me Slim."
"Why you never sucked my dick Steph? You too good? I mean, you can fuck me at the spot and shit. What's up?""
"I don't be going around suckin' no niggas dick."
"Where this shit you popping off at the mouth coming from then?"
"What?"
"Shit, I can get my dick sucked all night if I want. You gonna do something!"
"You gonna do something?" as I knelt on the bed, leaning over her shoulders.

Me Tears

"Come on."
  "You come on. I ain't never do no shit like that in my life. You betta get the fuck out of here."
"Come on Steph," rubbing myself on her. "Come on, I'll show you how. I'll show you how." Waiting. "Fuck it then."
  "Fuck it then," she said.
"Look, I'm out."
  "Stop playing," pulling me back.
Laying on my back, Steph rolled over on top of me.
"Get the fuck off me, for real."
  "How do I do it?"
"What do you mean?"
  "You want me to or not?"
"Word? Stop front'in."
  "For real."
"I don't know, I ain't never do no shit like that. They just do it. Just do it. Don't bite my ass though. I ain't wash it sense we were together that night that I asked you the last time."
  "Stop play'in."
"I ain't. Yo' ass gonna pick up where we left off. When I see Sheila tomorrow, I am gonna ask her and she will, and don't give

a fuck about wether I washed or not or been with you or not. Shit, If she handles her business, I might even kiss her ass. I don't be doing no shit like that."

"You never kiss me."

"Word."

"You gonna kiss some bitch that goes around sucking niggas dicks?" She looked shock.

"Turn off the television......Wait, I got it."

She wasn't a pro or anything. I got pro-'brain' before. To tell the truth, she was upsetting the hell out of me. I wasn't with this shit. Then, she thought I was going to kiss her ass. I had to turn to the side after I pulled her up from down there. I had to get me off.

"It's there?"

"What? Look, I don't eat no pussy and I don't be tonguing no broads.......word."

"You gonna treat me like them tricks out there?"

"Yo, I ain't never kiss no chick......you know."

"What you gonna do?"

"What the fuck with all this question shit?"

"You know Queen and Blee seeing each other and they kiss."

Me Tears

"That's them. Don't be putting me in their business and shit."

"Okay, okay, but we tight. You know how me an Queen is, and he be going down and shit."

"Well, that's y'all, and that's them, this is Slim shit right the fuck here. Respect that."

"It's gonna be like that?"

"Yo, back it up....come on now."

"I ain't playing with you Slim."

"What? Damn," Steph got on all fours, and made things work for me. We didn't talk much for the rest of the night. I did end up spending the night. I regretted that shit. Then, the morning brought about other people into my life.

"No, he right here," she was telling someone. It had to be Queen on the phone. "Slim, Slim....phone."

"Phone?" She put the phone to my ear, and gave me a kiss on the lips. I felt like choaking her.

"You betta stand up nigga," it was Queen.

"What?"

"Don't be play'in my sister like that either nigga."

"Word nigga," It was Blee. "Ha, ha, What

is up lay-her, play-her." I could hear him in the background.

"Move," Queen was back to the phone.

"Ask him if it was what he expected.," Blee yelled. "Shit nawh! Tell that nigga that."

"What? Put her on the phone."

"Shit nawh, you heard what I said."

"That nigga sick," Blee laughed.

"I ain't with this hijack a nigga shit. Fuck that." Steph snatched the phone.

"Yeah, I heard him......Anyway."

"Yo, check that nigga sis'," I could hear Queen.

"Check this cock bitch." I rolled out the bed.

"You heard that," Steph laughed.

When I came back from the bathroom, Steph started some more shit. I knew it was Queen talking.

"You gonna do me back now?"

"Back what?"

"You know."

" I know you ain't talking 'bout no eating no pussy."

"Why? What's up?"

"You betta get the fuck out my face with

Me Tears

that shit. Blee can eat all the pussy he want. I told you about that shit. My name is S-L-I-M. You betta check your sistah, for real."

That was the end of that conversation.

Watching Crewcats Work The Block

    We were promoted in-full, sort of. It wasn't long before shit began to happen. Our days of relaxing came to an end. We had to start watching muthas. Then one night, like a television seen, the 'jake' began popping up from nowhere. It was like the sun came out in the middle of the night. The lights were like heaters. They put all types of shit on us. Thangs were bouncing from off the pavement like hail in a sleet storm.
    The fellas, with the heat, for the most part hauled ass. That was the most important thing. We all knew the routine, none of that shit was ours. If fact we couldn't see shit. Them shits was there and was none of our damn business. The crew knew the drill. The resident base heads were my only concern. Now, I knew exactly why the lion hates the buzzard and other scavengers so damn much. The regular customers started to pace back and forth asking what the fuck is going on. They knew. "Get the fuck from around here," I told a few, and even though I could

Me Tears

do them cats at anytime, they were only concerned about right now. They didn't care that it was our product. It wasn't in our hands. It was like Christmas as they started to walk with energy, not dragging ass like the usual. The noise must have been like the Fourth of July to their ears. Base heads must pray for shit like this to happen. They knew we needed them.

My crew was all along the street and upside houses and bent over cars, the whole nine. The Stab niggas just walked the dogs like they didn't know anything. They didn't touch the Six to Six spot. That's where I was watching shit from the porch. Not one of us went in that night. A few of the crew got smacked up a bit. A few sat in the back of cars while warrants and shit were searched. The worst we got that night was trespassing and loitering. Out of nowhere those that went popped back up a couple hours later, but it didn't stop anything. The Stab and them took care of that type thing. It was like a bill, charged to the organization. There was no retribution for stuff like that.

"You muthafuckas bend over once, and that's your ass."

"What? What's up man? We cool

Me Tears

bro—What happened?" It was one of the base-heads.

"Go 'head and fuck up."

"Yo dawg, just trying to help a brother help a brother."

There was no way we could pick that shit up, and we couldn't sit watching all night either. They parked cars on all four corners. We were flexible, we moved over a couple of blocks and caught custies coming through yards and things. I didn't have time to fuck around with these cats, and something had to be done. I hated negotiating with these niggas.

"Yo man, we ain't got no choice unless you want to leave them shits."

"Fuck no," Blee said.

Blee was business. He hurt, having to work with these base heads.

"I work for you Blee," one of them begged.

"I got you Blee. You know I got you Blee," another said. Either way, we were beat. Shit never comes back right with a base head.....never.

"Yo, go 'head wit that shit nigga. You ghosts don't work for my ass-word. You niggas start picking up, and if shit come

Me Tears

back light. That's your ass muthafucka."
"What's our split Blee?'
 "Two for Ten."
"Four for ten dawg. Come on Blee that shit is hot. Them police right the fuck over there man." Looking around like he had a secret.
 "Muthafucka, two for ten bitch." I could understand Blee' thinking. Had he said five, they would have taken seven. Keeping it at two, he may get five.
 "Bet, bet. I'm just saying," as he rubbed his pockets.
"All my shit too. Then, we settle."
 "A hundred brings twenty right?"
"Word," They didn't see any police after that. Worst of all, there were no police in the first place. But, they see shit all the time. You never know.
   Only half of what we dropped came back to us that night. But, whatever, that was a positive. It was better than losing everything. It wasn't even two in the morning. Only about four hours after the police came and went. Then, those same two cats that picked up came back asking for hook ups. At the same time some of our soldiers were asking for mercy. They

Me Tears

had to make up for that lost, so they thought. They were never clear of that, they always owed for that. It kept them in check. All of those things that we got back from those base heads became ours in a since.   Once we left the block, those ghosts were coming out again. We knew they hid some shit and seen some shit that they didn't pick up. But, we couldn't watch over the shit all night.   That's that buzzard shit. The phone began to ring as well. The boss and them heard about things, but they weren't coming around, and that was for sure.

    The soldiers pleaded with Blee to give them at least a few things back. Blee acted like he had no idea of what they were talking about. I knew he was going to get his dick as limp as possible at the end of the shift from a few broads he knew.

"Why the fuck your ass was sleeping. You should have seen them muthafuck'n police," he answered them throughout the night.

"Wait until Tray get wind. Y'all niggas did." Blee was messing with them as he pulled on his weed, looking to the sky, exhaling.

Me Tears

"Why the fuck should we care about your ass anyway. You knew what this shit was about," I added.

"Word Blee, I got your back dawg, word," one of the crew said.
"Got my back? Yo, you hear this shit?" Looking at me.

"With what nigga? Back w'it what? You ain't even got your back."
"I'll hook you up-word."

"Word?" Blee asked.
"Word-man-word," he pleaded.

"Say word-the -fuck up," passing me the joint, exhaling.
"Word the fuck up Blee," he said

"Word? Uncle? Fo-ril?" Blee added.
"Word Uncle Blee."

"Nawh, say for-r'il" pulling another hit.
"For realllllll," the cat begged.

"I don't know 'bout yo' ass son. Niggas say all types shit in times like this and right before they get smoked and shit. You ever watch that nigga on the Godfather before they popped him?"

"Paulie or some shit," I added.
"Yeah, that muthafucka."

"Remember that nigga?" Blee asked

Me Tears

him.

"Tell him man," he looked a me.

"Fo r'il," Blee looked at me.

"Shit, I don't know this nigga like that. I ain't co-signing shit."

"Fo-r'il dawg."

"Fo-r'il For real?" Blee asked.

"For real, For real Blee."

" Why for real, for real now? Straight up."

"You said for real."

"Whateva son."

"Word Blee, Whateva, Whatevea Blee."

"Word to Who?"

"Word to Whoeva Blee, Fo' r'il Fo r'il cousin"

"Cousin? See this shit?"

" I meant uncle, word Blee."

"Your Miz?"

"My Miz Blee, Word up Uncle Blee, for real Uncle Blee. To my Miz Uncle Blee-Word."

"On JBlack? On JBlack?" Blee asked out of the corner of his eyes.

"JBlack, word to JBlack Blee- Word," he said. JBlack had been hit about two months earlier.

"Your sister. Say word to JBlack and I can

Me Tears

fuck your sister."

"What sister man? I ain't got no sister."

"Ebonica"

"That ain't my sister man. But, you can fuck her. I'll help-word."

"Word to life?"

"Word to life Blee-Uncle Blee man."

Blee then gave him the two hundred worth he was short. Oct along with Trap were the only two that got a play that night. He only helped that nigga out because he was the cat that had his cousin Trap's back. They came in together.

All the next day, crew was asking each other what the deal was gonna be. Some of them never dropped shit before, but they knew about 'Them Niggas'. Oct told Blee some of them soldiers were gonna skip out of town and shit because they couldn't sleep. They were having bad dreams, 'Them Niggas' was gonna come and get them. "What's What?" is all they would ask each other all day. Which was usually answered

"I don't know cousin. Y'all fucked up dawg," the Stab was enjoying this shit. They would have them guys on point all week. Soldiers were going to the store,

Me Tears

and buying them shit all week. They were like servants, not workers, because each time they took a break they would do something for the Stab if they needed. It gave them a chance to ask about 'Justice', and What's What about them thangs.

They were okay on payday. Everyone was peace, as the payroll came back right as usual. That's because the report was true. Niggas couldn't help that shit. No one got missing.

Me Tears

Queen

As I came to know Queen a bit better, I understood she wasn't a mean or bad person. She was simply doing and being what she was taught. Ragga, and Tray taught her everything she knew about the life. *During her adolescent her job was to hold the cash, and stack for Ragga and Tray in the early days. She didn't have a father except for the two of them. After school she was watching them trying to come up. She saw how they would take the tricks and such in the basement during the summer when they would come over to her and her mother's home.*

They weren't real brothers and sisters. Their father, was poking her and Steph mother. Queen and Steph never had a father in their life. Ragga, Tray, nor their father really cared for women in a manner of speaking. Tray, he only made sure they got what they wanted as form of payment to them for helping him do his fledgling street hustle.

It is possible that Queen may have very well seen Ragga do what she later did to

Me Tears

my dawg across the street that night. There was no need to tell anything to Ragga or Tray. That was like signing your own death warrant. Sometimes they had to spend time together because of their father's relationship with their mother.

    It was easy to understand the bond that they had. They just couldn't trust anyone. They went through that part of the eighties when niggas were just getting popped at will because of the new crack thing going on. In those days, all you had was family. There was too much money, and niggas didn't know how to act. Everyone knew how to handle weed, that was slow shit. When crack came out, there was so much more money, and if you could picture the way a base head moved versus someone smoking weed you can understand going from mellow to chaos.

Me Tears

BLEE'S COUSIN

    That's the problem with mistakes. Someone has to pay for them. I knew Blee was going to give his little cousin some play that night. Blee was like a father to him although few of the crew knew what that meant. He was only thirteen or fourteen. He had a small frame, black as tar brotha, with a worn grill Blee gave him. He always got shit that Blee passed down. Old kicks, and jackets, or whatever. It's not that he couldn't get new shit. He was smart enough to know that when fellas saw him with Blee's shit on, they were looking at Blee, and to know Blee, he just didn't give niggas on the block shit. He didn't fuck with niggas like that.
    Blee would get pissed off at times with Trap, his cousin, because he broke a lot of Blee's gear. Not that he fucked it up or anything, he would just come on the block from time to time with some of Blee's stuff on that Blee wasn't done with yet. Blee would have to get a whole new joint. It didn't matter if Blee jacked the little nigga up in front of the crew neither. The little

Me Tears

cat would just say: "Yeah man, heard you man." Blee knew it was about respect for Trap. Everyone knew that Blee was the only one who could do some shit like that to Trap. That little nigga would put one in your ass.

I found out what a nice side my dawg Blee had to him one night. He actually did have a heart. One summer night in late summer, we were on a night off on the porch chillin', smokin'. When Queen and Steph found us, that's found because Blee began letting Queen get hit off more on a regular. This was a few months after she first met him for real. When they got out of the car other cats began to spread out, but not Trap. Steph came close to me without making a first move, she usually didn't outside.

"So, you think about what I said?" The question was for Blee.

"What?"

"Don't even Blee, for real," She rolled her eyes. Steph came closer to me as Trap passed Blee the joint. I looked at Steph, like 'What?'

"Play Wha....Ma, Damn."

"We rollin' together or what?"

"Go 'head, you know you the Wi-Fee."

Me Tears

"You know what I mean. You know how I'm feeling you Blee."

"Y'all need some privacy or something. I can't tell if I'm watching a movie or some shit. This weed is blaze dawg. Is this some personal type shit? You fucking up my high." I cut my eyes at Blee, smiling.

"Oh, shit funny?" Queen smiled as Blee smiled.

"Nawh, you my Queen, Queen. Come on now, chill baby."

"You love me?" She asked. She was bold like that. That was some personal type shit. I didn't want to hear my dawg say 'yes' to that shit.

"I love you. Fuck this nigga," Trap said, as he stepped to Queen.

"Oh shit. Now that's a man," Steph said. "You don't need this muthafucka Queen. I love, love you," resting his head to her breast. "We don't need these muthafuckas Queen," as he reached around an rubbed her ass. She didn't move an inch, ignoring Trap.

"Say it," She stared at Blee.

"I'll put one in his ass right now Queen. For you baby." Trap looked at Blee and put his finger to his dome.

Me Tears

"You betta not be saying you love my chick, word," looking up at Queen. "He ain't gonna do you right. I know that nigga. He for self. I'll give you the world Queen." Steph started to laugh, as Blee put his head in his hands.

"This little nigga can up it and you can't? That's where we at now?" Queen pushed Trap away, and stepped closer to the porch. Trap wasn't finished as he became a pest, rapping his arms around Queen from behind.

"Fuck that nigga baby, fuck him," Trap moaned. I was wishing it was me grinding that ass.

"What do you want with this?" Queen stepped closer to Blee, and Trap stepped with her with little baby steps shadowing her. His little ass couldn't let go. I understood.

When she got close enough to the step and reached over for Blee she had to bend at the waist and her short enough mini-skirt came up a bit and Trap still wouldn't let go.

"No baby, he's all damn it wrong," Trap whispered to Queen. It was like he wasn't there. Then, he started to grind a bit from behind.

Me Tears

"Would you tell this nigga to get his dick from my ass?"

"Go 'head Trap," Blee smacked him, but he didn't let go.

"Trap-man," Queen started to laugh.

"Say it. Then I'll let go. I love you Queen. He can't say it," Trap looked at Blee.

"Diddo damn it," Blee said.

"What the fuck is Diddo?"

"What the nigga said?" Steph said.

"Hey, hey," I nudged Steph.

"Sound like the nigga said dildo," Trap said, as everyone laughed.

"Diddo-word," I smiled, giving Blee some knuckles.

"Diddo muthafucka. It means 'same here', you ignorant muthafucka." That nigga made me proud.

Me Tears

Queen Gets Pregnant

Blee had been seeing Queen for a while. They sort of broke up or something especially while Blee was seeing that chick from around the projects. Queen had sense enough to cut off most of them other hooches. Both of them, she and Steph spent a lot of their time posting up on our spot. Blee was calm when it came to Queen and was spitting some slick shit, if you know what I mean. He would slide on his belly to that other broad . But, she couldn't get much of his time while Queen was around.

Then one day, we were siting at the spot and Queen hauled off and smacked Blee. The nigga was calm and all. There wasn't too much he could do, especially with Tray and Ragga along with Them Niggas around. Most of the crew looked. The Stab, they laughed. Queen was serious as a woman could be. Blee, he went to the bar for a shot and a brew. Everyone could tell shit wasn't usually like that. Queen never lost it like that, she could give a damn about crew niggas. I

Me Tears

only knew it was some other woman type shit. Come to find out later, I was wrong. "Let's bounce dawg," he said as I smiled and watched the drip of red from the corner of his mouth. He wasn't the type to get excited by some shit like that. He was proactive in getting excited, he didn't react like that. Hell, I knew he seen it coming. He didn't bother to duck, put a hand up or nothing. I took a double shot and followed him to the door. Queen threw a drink at him as he passed, and some caught me as well.

"Boss, Boss, Boss," he looked at the table where Tray and the others were and nodded. "I'm out," he added, I echoed him.

We got to the door and no sooner had he pulled out some smoke.

"Gimme some fire."
"Yo! What was that shit nigga?"
"You know how them Ho's is."
"What? You told her 'bout some other bitch or something?"
"Nawh dog."
"Oh, you just broke up-up with the chick?"
"Shit, I wish. She pregnant dawg?"
"What? What?" I laughed, bending over.
"Oh shit."

Me Tears

"She trying to give that shit to me. I ain't having it." He inhaled.

"Yo Blee, she ain't been seeing nobody else." "Say word nigga."

"You right. You never can tell dawg."

"Did it look like bullshit? 'Cause it damn sure didn't feel like bullshit when she swung on my ass."

"Shit nigga, you a baby daddy?" Queen ain't no bad wi-fee nigga."

"What?"

"She said she told me first, but I bet she is in that bitch telling Tray and them already. Shit, I ain't claiming shit."

"You was claiming that shit for weeks when you was fucking her ass. Nigga pass that shit. Don't let that personal shit fuck up your two totes and pass skills. I know you shook and all, but damn, get a grip nigga. Now what? You don't recognize the pussy. Betta recognize nigga. What you tell her?" He was toting, shaking his head.

"Who the daddy?" He laughed, and I laughed with him, giving the nigga some palm.

"Word?"

"Word nigga."

"Oh no...Nigga you betta go back and

Me Tears

clean that shit up. Claim your youth son, and pass that shit before I smack you."
"You crazy as fuck nigga, shit."
"Word Blee, Tray a uncle now nigga, you the nigga now, son."
"I don't give a fuck."
"Yo dawg, she didn't just up and get swollen nigga," laughing.
"What? Who the fuck side is you on. Steph got your ass whipped to that?"
"You 'bout to be in like a muthafucka nigga....word. Pass the shit man."
"What the fuck...."
"Go back in that bitch. Come on nigga while the fire hot dawg. You gotta go back and fess-up and tell the chick you down. Then, you be all the way down. You be one of "Them Niggas" I could see his mind wording, as he froze.
"Word?"
"Word dawg. That type nigga now. What the fuck is wrong with you? You know that shit is yours."
"Nigga you say that shit again, I will bust your ass."
"Yo, Yo. Tray there, everyone there nigga. Ain't nobody expecting your ass to be calm and cool like that, after that, and

Me Tears

go back and step to that chick. Shit, it would fuck my mind up and I'm the nigga that already know dawg," he started to laugh.

"Word?"

"Muthafucka you need to carry your stupid ass back up in there. You already won the lotto, get the prize....shit, and pass the muthafucka man, damn."

"Word?"

"Step up to the plate. Shit, when you see the head, you'll know if the little nigga yours."

"Word nigga?"

"If you wait it will be too damn late. You either on her side or not. Tray on her side. Where that leaves you? Think nigga. Shit, he down with Queen whateva nigga. You ain't the daddy, Tray be the daddy. Once that nigga the daddy, you ain't never gonna be the daddy, and that's word."

"Word-huh?" Blee smiled and shook his head.

"Out that shit. Pass that shit man. Marry that chick."

"Fuck that Shit."

"Well, go claim. Do something. Don't be stupid. You know what? I'm about to go

Me Tears

claim that baby my damn self. Fuck you son." Blee turned around and didn't say a word as we walked back a half block or more to the spot. When we stepped inside, all eyes were on him as everyone shut the hell up. For all anyone knew, he could start spraying niggas. He knew not to make any sudden moves, as he stepped over to Steph and Queen sitting in the booth with Tray looking down at Queen as she rolled her eyes.
"What you want?"
"Yo, Don't be pranking on me Queen aiight? That's word. You say whateva, whateva then, word. I ain't 'bout the bullshit though," he then looked at Tray. "Yo, peace boss," who nodded up at the cat. Blee checked out as fast as he stepped in. As I followed, Tray's eyes got serious as his brows came together. I stopped as I was about to give him props and shit.

    Queen slid out and followed behind Blee.

  "Oh shucks," Steph said, as Queen smiled, trying to hold it back.
"Whateva bitch", she replied.
I knew Blee was gonna be in shock, thinking it was me coming out the door

Me Tears

behind him only finding out it was Queen. But, I had my own drama to contend with.

"What next nigga?" Tray said looking at me. He continued.

"That nigga ain't got sense enough to pull shit off like that. That nigga a thug for real, a trigga nigga. You what? That was you right?" Looking, chewing on his chew stick.

"Nawh, Blee his own shit man."

"Okay, Okay," smiling back at me.

"Word Boss-man."

"Sit yo' ass down," as Ragga smiled and tilted his head to the side.

"Right here," Steph moved over.

"Hey, I didn't know nothing about this pregnant shit."

"You fucking Steph?"

"Uh-what?"

"Did the rest of y'all hear the question or is it me?"

"I heard," Ragga smiled.

"Tell the truth, that's why I like your ass. You know how to dummy-the-fuck-up. But for real, you fucking my sistah?"

"Boss, that's the nigga out there with his hands in the damn cookie jar. You pregnant or something. I don't mean or

Me Tears

something (looking at Steph). You are either pregnant or you aren't. Not that it is any of my concern." looking at Steph, with my hand to my chest.
"So.....That's a 'no'?" Ragga asked.
"Do I have to put one in this muthafucka or what to get a straight answer?" looking at Steph, who was smiling.
  "She makes me boss."
"She makes you what? Fuck her?"
  "She makes your dick get hard? That's what the fuck this nigga saying," looking at Ragga, as Steph laughs.
"Shit. don't look at me. She don't make my shit hard."
  "She is the boss, you know."
"She rapes your bitch ass?"
  "Yeah, yeah, like they say on TV. I say no. But, she keeps on, you know."
"Where does this shit happen?"
  "Everywhere," leaning forward.
"You call the police or some shit," Steph couldn't take it any more, and I started to laugh with her.
"Get the fuck outta here man," Ragga started to shake his head.
  "See, you believe that shit?"
"I like that nigga." Tray said, as me and

Me Tears

Steph left the table, wasting no time. "What the fuck....," I heard Tray laugh.

    I must admit, I wasn't far from a nervous breakdown. I headed straight to the bar. From Blee busting up in the joint, and seeing Them Niggas look as if they were gonna pull. I could only try to find a spot to run to or someone to get close enough to catch some of the fire. Mamma knows I would have used any one of them brothas as a human shield. They pack some heavy heat. Then, to have Tray question me about his sister. That was too much stress. But, getting up successfully from that table without even a smack or nothing did something. Niggas in the crew had to spread out and recognize and respect that shit. With that baby Queen was baking, I knew me and my boy was about to come up. That brotha was my right hand. I felt as if I could just smack someone right 'bout now. And get away with it.

    It wasn't but a few minutes before I had to leave. I went outside to check on Blee's situation, but he was out. Steph came up from behind me.

"Go on Steph," I smiled, and pushed her hands away.

Me Tears

"Come on Slim," Steph moaned, pulling from behind.

"Stop before your peeps come the fuck out here. That's how shit start."

"What start baby? The rape?" laughing.

"Not now...fuck nawh," as she started to laugh more.

"He already knew.......damn. If he didn't like your ass, you would know by now."

"I don't want no baby."

"What? What Slim? What you saying?"

"Whatever Queen does, yo'ass does, and you gonna want to do the baby thing too."

"I always wanted a baby."

"You need to get a nigga that wants that then."

"What?"

"I ain't trying to hear no shit like that..word."

"I love you Slim. Come on."

"Go 'head with that Steph."

"Fuck it then," Steph threw her arms up and started to walk to the car.

"Where you going BabyGirl?"

"You know what? If I didn't say shit. I would have been a bitch for just putting one on you and shit. Right?" Her hands

Me Tears

were on her hips, leaning to me, staring me in the eyes.
  "What you saying?"
"Will you marry me then damn it? 'Cause I love you Slim, and I want a baby of my own. There... Or are you with the bullshit?"
  "Married?"
"Yeah nigga," it was Blee, and Queen coming from the side of the building.
"Y'all heard that shit?"
"Couldn't help but hear that shit."
"Ain't this some crazy shit. You a daddy, and I'm the nigga tracked for marriage," as I put my arm about Blee who was laughing. "That would make the nigga what? Best man. He don't look like no best man to me."   Queen's arms went up and both her and Steph were screaming and hugging each other.
"Look at 'em," Blee said.
  "I'm tired of this shit man. Muthafuckas trying to run niggas lives and shit."
"Somebody knows how to step up to the plate," Steph rolled her eyes.
  "What he said?" Queen nodded in my direction.
    "What the fuck you looking at? He said

Me Tears

'no'," I answered as Steph folded her arms as if she was gonna cry. Queen was talking like I couldn't hear her ass.

"Go 'head man. Stop with the fingering me man. This your man right here," pointing at Blee.

"You go 'head nigga." I replied.

"Yo' ass getting late nigga."

"Look we are getting married, we doing the damn thing-thing nigga. Queen said it was cool," Blee stated.

"Con-gra-tu-fuck-in-la- tions my dawg," I gave Blee some love.

"Yeah, you too nigga. Tray blessed us all."

"What all?"

"You don't have to," Steph said.

The door opened and out came Tray and them.

"Congrats, Congrats," Tray gave Blee some dap. Then, me.

"Bet boss," Blee said.

"He ain't fo' sho'," Queen pointed at me. Tray started to laugh, for real this time.

"This is my nig, for real. You deny shit boy don't you? Damn. Can you get fo' sho? We need you to get fo' sho'. Steph needs fo' sho', and your boy here needs fo'

Me Tears

sho'. Y'all got to go through this shit together man. Y'all together man," as he laughed.

"What?" Blee looked at me in shock. "If you don't wanna tie the knot nigga I ain't mad at you. Word, I understand. But, I don't want no shit from the two of you. Husband and wife shit, that's your business. But, if you two fuck up my business, then that's my business. Maybe you don't want to be a part of my immediate family, that's cool. Much love," Tray stepped off, patting me on the shoulder, followed by Them Niggas patting me on the shoulder. I could feel the pressure, even though it was a slight touch. It was like the Mafia guy in the Godfather getting a kiss from one of them cats before they got rid of his ass.
"No disrespect. I ain't no good with this love shit man. She said she loves me. You know? She asked me to make a baby man." Tray turned.
"Fucking and making a baby is the same shit. You know baby is coming with the one, you don't know with the other. You ask me nigga, you got a better deal than that nigga," referring to Blee. { putting his hand on my shoulder}.

Me Tears

"Look, them two been planning this shit for ever since I can remember. You just fell into this shit. You know like walking down the street and a nigga mistake you for someone and start bucking at your ass." One of Them Niggas smiled, nodding his head.

"This ain't your fault Slim. But, shit would be a lot better with everything if you were a team player. Sometimes you have to suck one up for the team. The team needs you. Sure, we can get a substitute or something. You know, someone off the bench. But, nothing like being in the starting line-up. Maybe you a bench player," he smiled.

"Nawh, I'm straight. I got it boss." I didn't know if he meant kill my ass for that 'bench' remark or what. Substitute, what the fuck did that shit mean? It didn't feel good.

"How easy is life? Damn right you straight nigga. All you have to do is be at the church. Steph gonna tell you what to wear. That shit starts before you even get married. Didn't you know that, or you still not fucking her? Shit. The reverend gonna say his shit, and all you have to do is be on time and say "I do". Shit, imagine

Me Tears

what I have to decide each day. You married, you don't have to think any more son. You damn right you straight," as he laughed walking away.

"Shit, or never think again. You have two 'never think agains' to choose from dawg," Blee smiled.

"Punk ass," looking at Blee.

"Burgundy, Peach, What girl?' they started to hug each other.

"Look at this shit. I told you to wear a fucking hat on that dick nigga."

"Y'all muthafuckas wasn't worrying about the milk. Now you got the cow."

"See, this shit already started. Look at the rest of your life nigga, look." looking at Queen.

"Oh cheer up Slim."

"I ain't marrying you unless you love me Slim."

"Love you? I ain't got shit to do with this shit."

"Yeah, you the victim."

"Say it," Queen nudged Steph, pushing her to me.

"Go 'head," Blee said, smiling.

"I know Dildo, I mean, dido man ain't talking. Look at what the fuck you done

Me Tears

did man," walking away.
"Hold up Dawg. Yo-I holla Queen."
as the two of us disappeared down the alley.

Worthy

    Worthy came out and that's when shit got burning on the block. Him and a few other cats from the old school thought they should have gotten more than they had been given. It's not that they didn't respect the work that Tray and Steph and them did. They just wasn't the business type. They didn't understand the survival of the family. They were just brothas for the survival of themselves. I guess the cell block teaches you that. Shit, I don't know. I only know that Worthy and Ragga had words.
    They didn't like each other over some broad type shit from way back in the day. Then, they didn't know who the baby daddy was. Shit, like that shit matters now. The hooch got two or three more babies now and none of them want her.
    You could smell brothas taking sides. Elf remained on the block. But, was

Me Tears

watched. He was suspect to the Chiefs and the crew as well, being related and all. He was given a post away from the spot, and didn't get to stay on the block too much. He ran back and forth a lot. We were hinted to not speak about business with him because of his associations with Worthy and Cuz. But, you never can tell who be talking to who. They knew some shit was gonna happen, we knew it too. Tray was smart enough to begin the house cleaning once he found out that some of the people down with Cuz was going to try something. He began with the brotha Queen was seeing a couple of niggas ago after she broke up with Cuz.

The Park

Sometimes things happen. But, I wasn't the type brother that believe in that coincident type shit. I remember this day just as if it was yesterday.
We were all mandated to be at the park, that is, the people that weren't at the bottom of the 'so called' pecking order. Early in the morning, the neighborhood kids at summer basketball and sports in the park and we were a big part of that. We

Me Tears

sponsored them.

It was gonna be a hot day. It was already about eighty or so and it was just ten in the morning. People were in the park not associated with the games. A few were jogging around the track. We were well situated in the joint. Most of the Stab were there with their dogs, and the other brothers had without doubt, the heat.

Then, out of nowhere, or should I say from the track, those brothers on the track, and a chick started to fire. Along with them were some ass-holes on the other side of the fence to our back. All we could do was get down. The children got down too. None of them were hit. Thank goodness for the dogs. The Stab let them go, and they started to do work. One of them were shot, and the others ran those cats off from the track. That is, the ones that managed to get over the fence on the far side of the park. One of the niggas didn't make it.

At first, he was being handled by one of the dogs. Then when the cats jumped the fence, the other dogs joined in on his ass. It was difficult to tell how many times he got bit. He was alive, you could hear him yelling, and screaming. The Stab formed a

Me Tears

circle. There were about twenty of them dogs out that day. Not one of them made the dogs stop.

Then, you heard nothing. You couldn't see anything either. The dogs were the only one making sounds, the growling eating a nigga ass sound. Eventually, they called them off but it was too late. You couldn't recognize the body. It was too bloody. Raz said it was Pimp. If it were Pimp, Cuz had something to do with it. Even though he was in jail, he had reach.

Tray had gotten hit a couple of times and was bleeding on the ground. We didn't know how bad he got hit at first. The kids that were there, had all ran from the park. The Stab disappeared, all but three, and a few of the dogs remained.

I ambulance and police showed up. Tray was already on his way to the hospital. They got a few of the crew. They weren't moving on the ground at all. They looked dead. Most cats that were hot took off. Other brothas took steel and left before the police got there. They got off a few shots, and word was out for any hit niggas. We wanted to know exactly what it was that brought this heat.

Two of our people didn't make it. Tray

Me Tears

was hurt up sort of bad with a chest and shoulder shot. We had to shut the block down for the rest of the day. We were still out, just not working. Them Niggas stayed in place at the hospital with the hit people. Ragga disappeared and Queen appeared on the block with Steph. They were all shook. But, in my mind it was no time to fuck around.

"Yo, Y'all get them chicks of yours out here," I told Queen and Steph.

"What do you mean?" Steph asked.

"Yo, just get on the damn phones and call your chicks and tell them to get off their ass and get the fuck over here. Now! Queen, you need to tell them Stab niggas to stay off the block. They can still handle their business otherwise, just not out here. Not today." Neither Queen or Steph had shit to say about it.

Queen and Steph began to heat up the phones. Within an hour or so. Most of the tricks were on the block, and they were matched up with the crew that were on the block. They were matched up just as if they were girlfriend and boyfriend not drug dealers and hookers.

The next move was simple. Each pair of them were brought to one of our

Me Tears

apartments around the spot. All of those cats that just got out or was out a minute and had people in one of our apartments were kicked the fuck out on the streets. It was no time to try and sort out who was who. Shit was real, and all of our ass could have been locked up. One thing for sure, the chicks weren't gonna say anything, and the crew didn't know anything. Queen and Steph understood once I explained to them.

The move was strong. We needed to know who were in the houses around the spot while we worked for one. Secondly, those women of Steph and Queen would throw that ass on those young boys in the crew running the block. I knew they never had pussy like that. For sure, the first thing they would want to do once they got off of work would be go home, and those girls were ordered to do whatever. As long as they were occupied like that, they weren't gonna get in any trouble, and stay in the house, not talking to anyone but the chicks. They thought they were in love. They were going to be just like the crack heads once this shit was over, pussy heads, strung the fuck out, whipped.

Ray-Ray was one of the two brothers that stayed in his shit. I remember when he

Me Tears

came home from jail. He was always about the business.

His baby momma was seeing some other cat from somewhere else. We didn't believe in taking a brother out over no pussy. His ex wanted to stay with the man she was screwing around with. The mother tried to convince her to cut the nigga off. But, the chick decided to move the hell out. The mother had other plans. When Ray-Ray told her to get out, the mother had different ideas.

"Shit, I ain't the one that was fucking that nigga. This my grandson here. Ain't no need of him getting his life all turned upside down because his momma want to go running after some nigga. I tried to tell her to cut that nigga off. Don't let some other nigga raise your baby Ray. I'll watch him for you. Why should I leave? I ain't do shit."

That's all Ray needed to hear. He kept his son, and that was that. The grandmother wasn't trying to leave a hook-up like that. She had no bills to pay and had everything any woman needed or wanted in a house.

Once a woman can call a plumber, electrician, or exterminator and they come,

Me Tears

that's it. Tray made sure they came. Ain't no way you can get them to go back to the housing project to put up with all them roaches and niggas raising hell all the time. That would be like trying to throw a cat in the water twice. The grandma wasn't that bad either. Ray started hittin' that ass just as if he loved her, and she loved it.

Tray pulled through, and we attended the memorial for the fallen. Shit calmed down. Steph and Queen, along with Ragga in the distant background hunting down some niggas, ran the show for a while. I was a very silent partner in the matter. I thought up all the different plans, and kept the physical block in order. Steph had niggas fall in line. I had Blee just in case. He was screaming and itching to pop a mutha on account of JB being one of those niggas that got smoked.

It didn't last long, the shake up of things and all. Tray came back as if nothing happened, and Ragga began to show his face as well. A few brothas that were down with Pimp before the incident became missing. We knew who did the shit, sort of. Needless to say, Worthy, Elf and a couple of other cats were never heard from again.

Me Tears

Disappearing Act

After things became what they did. Tray and Ragga were hardly seen. They left things to their sisters. Most times the two brothers were simply absent. Rawga was going to be getting strong as the months dragged on. Cuz was going to be out in a bit. He wasn't going to appreciate the changes in life. He was locked down about three on a twelve bid. Worst of all, Queen stopped visiting him three years ago, it was said.

One morning on a Saturday, she popped up to the upstate. She usually went on a Sunday for open visits but she got word. Someone was visiting Cuz, his baby momma or something. There was no drama in the visiting room. When Steph and Queen popped up, that other chick hauled ass.

Queen had went to the officer at the front desk and when they called Shanique, the other chick for the visit, Steph and Queen let her know. She didn't know who Queen was. Anyhow, Shanique left, and Queen and Steph took the visit. But first,

Me Tears

they had the officer announce Shanique. When Queen came though the door, Cuz turned ghost-like. That was something I knew Tray or Ragga had something to do with. Niggas in the lock down talk and Tray and Ragga wasn't going to let Cuz play Queen like that. The closer he got to Queen the more dangerous he was. Not only which, Queen was Rawga. Queen was woman about her representation. She had a panther on her lower back, standing on the word RAWGA.

Blee said he was in shock the first time he saw her tattoo. He only saw it after they got married. He said, she didn't let him see it, because she never backed it up with the lights on, until they got married. Blee said it was one of the best pieces of art and ass in his life.

Queen was pissed at that Cuz brotha because she was holding it down for years without that cat. She kept dough on the books before and after they went their separate ways. She didn't go way up north anymore to see him. Blee was the only brother she got with now. But, before him she was ruthless, probably because of that Cuz nigga. She kept dough on the books for all them locked down niggas. That was

Me Tears

what she did for Rawga Crew. That was business. Cuz was just business now.

Word got around to Cuz upstate that Queen got married. Blee had no idea who the brotha was really, and didn't much care. He use to see him years earlier, but that's it. That didn't stop Cuz from sending word out that Queen was going to still be his when he got out. Steph didn't have that problem and didn't interfere.

Jam was her ex, and Jam, her former whatever ain't coming back in the picture. He was smoked. Both he and Steph were downtown and after they went shopping one day, Jam was sleeping on this cat from across town over some old beef he forgot about. When he came out of the store, some brotha caught him point blank to the dome. That's why Cuz was on lock when Steph told Tray and Rawga who popped Jam. They put the law of the jungle in effect, and hunted the brother before the police got him. Over a period of just a couple of months quite a few soldiers were lost. They shot on sight. Jam and Cuz were step-brothers. If it were up to Cuz, he would have went out blazin' the entire crew. For the sake of Rawga, he copped to the bid, although they say three of them

Me Tears

bodies were Ragga. Cuz took all three and the heat went away, as a truce was made after someone from the other crew copped to Jam.

    The worst part about this is that Cuz thinks that everyone on the outside was eating off of him and he sacrificed the world for everyone. Sure, his daughter and his baby momma was being taken care of. Tray helped them in getting a house and all. His ex, Molinda worked with the city. Tray gave her a piece of Cuz pie. His mother had a house she owned, right next door to his daughter and watched his daughter. It wasn't any of Rawga's fault she didn't want him anymore. It was never that serious. She lost Cuz to Queen and now that Queen was out of the picture, she wanted Cuz back anyway.

    There was no telling how things would turn out. Especially with a few other brothers coming out with Cuz. They weren't Rawga, but they were crew.

    Things started to grow a bit more tense when Cuz got out after being locked down for that bid. It's hard I guess trying to please a brotha after being out of the loop so long. For one, he didn't have Queen anymore, and probably thought that Tray

Me Tears

and Ragga had something to do with that. For two, Blee did, and it wasn't going to be no piece of cake trying to move that nigga neither. For Three, those brotha's now running the block were an entirely different crew. They were loyal to Ragga and Tray. Other cats remembered Cuz, but he was shiesty and the organization was a machine now.

There wasn't going to be any stunting on the block. The Stab would make sure of that. Those pits and rotties would make sure of that. Cuz was just another fella and not one person was gonna give up their spot on account. His only play was with Tray.

When he was given a sit down, not one person was surprised. It was better than a war, not that he could win. We all met at the spot. Cuz was with a few other cats and bounced up in the joint with this nigga named Pimp from the past days. His right hand, who got out last year. Pimp ain't have no heart without Cuz. Tray gave him little things to do, nothing major, nothing too close to the business.

Me Tears

The Spot

Blee strolled up on the spot with Queen, who just not long ago had their first child. They didn't say much, as Blee spoke to the table in general and Queen was on his arm. The Stab was in the house in full, with their dogs hanging outside, all over the damn place. Them Niggas was ready for whateva, as a few nodded at Queen and Blee as they took a squat in the corner away from Tray and Ragga. It was exceptional seeing them all at the same time. I never saw any shit like that.

When Steph came in, pregnant and shit, niggas were at ease, and she was the only cause for a relaxing smile. We didn't have to be hard for that, it was like breathing a breath of fresh air after all the stale shit going on in the house. I was hoping she would stay home, but she wasn't going to unless I stayed. Everyone knew that wasn't going to happen. But, as soon as she entered, I had to play the daddy role. We gave props to the table and all, but that was it. Issues were at hand.

As we sat at the table along side Blee

Me Tears

and Queen, shit stared.

"George got out I see," I started.

"That's the nigga's name?" Blee asked, like he didn't know.

"Yeah."

"I'm needing something to drink baby, the babies are thirsty."

"BabyGirl, you should have kept you and the baby home. Ya'll straight?" I asked Blee and Queen getting up to get my babies' drinks.

  "I don't like that nigga," Blee was looking towards Cuz while he rubbed his beard.

"Word!"

  "Oh, come on baby," Queen said.

"Shit, that nigga took Queen from me years ago."

  "Yo- man, what?"

"Yo, cut it out." Queen injected with her rolling eyes.

  "Yo, I'm just keeping it real. I was in love with Queen before any you niggas. That's right, that was way back in school. I came over to the crib one day, she swapping spit with that nigga."

"Word?"

  "Broke my fuckin' heart. Ask Steph. She knows. Now I got this," pointing at Steph,

Me Tears

as everyone at the table laughs.
"Can I get something to drink?"
 "Yo, can I get a minute?" It was Cuz, and he was speaking to Queen as if Blee wasn't there. Blee ignored the question as Queen looked up. Steph looked at me, and laughed.
 "Cuz what's up?" Steph asked her cousin.
"Yeah, what's up?"
"What minute? Can't you see I am with my husband?"
 "This is Blee, and Slim," Steph said.
"And What?" Cuz answered.
"This is my husband, and this is Blee, Queen's husband."
"And What?"
"Yo Dawg......." Blee started as one of the Stab came to the table.
"It's okay baby," Queen held Blee's hand.
"Nawh, you got a wish nigga? 'Cause I make shit like that come true.
"What?" Cuz countered.
"I know you probably got pieces of dick in your ass nigga, but I didn't know you have dick in your ears bitch." Blee stood, and I stood, and looking around, a lot of niggas started to stand. Them Niggas, along with

Me Tears

Tray and Ragga were the only people sitting. Shit got live.

It didn't take a second, never mind a second thought before Blee flipped his .380 to Cuz's temple.

"Say pull the trigger nigga," Blee whispered in the ear.

"Go head, say that shit. He'll do it," I begged. Then, he jabbed the nigga to the nose, and kicked him. Not one person said a word. Then, Blee stepped to the brotha with Cuz.

"You wanna say something to my wife too?"

"What? —What?"

"You can't hear bitch?" He put the piece to his ear.

"You need help hearing?" Then, Smack!!!!!

"Is there anyone else in the muthafucka that needs to speak to my wife?" Blee turned around looking at niggas. Then, he stepped to Cuz.

"Baby----," Queen tried.

"Not now," as Cuz was bleeding from the nose.

"Let me tell your bitch ass something nigga. I can't just go around just talking to chicks and shit. I would love to be able to

Me Tears

get some pussy, other niggas pussy. But, that's them muthafuckas reality. Hell, she might be watching niggas kick my ass right about now," as Blee kicked him. "Like that. This is a respectable place. So, I ain't gonna bust a cap in yo' ass. But, if you want to step the fuck outside. So, what I'm gonna do is take you outside and put one in your ass."

"Boss said enough Blee," one of Them Niggas said, as Blee looked to the table at Tray who gave him the slightest look, and nod.

"Shit," Blee said, and all of the Stab sighed a damn.

"Damn, I don't want my baby being around no shit like that," said Queen. "I told your ass to stay home."

"Let's get the fuck out," Blee said as we all got up and paid our respect to the table. "Yo boss......" Blee tried to say as we passed the table, and Queen pulled him.

Me Tears

The Call

"Tray wanna see you," Steph said waking me up.
" What happened now? Damn, I ain't do shit." I couldn't help but to slow my speech as I became distracted by the way she rolled over to me from hanging up the phone. Those beautiful hilltops of hers was a sight as I smiled looking up at them. "What is going on?" The block? I had my own dogs and a few fellas that I was in charge of. Blee got bumped up too. We didn't spent too much time on the block. We checked the Six to Six dough and things like that, along with going to the other side and things. We were more or less the male Queen and Steph now. All they did was shop and say shit like:
 "Oh girl this, and Oh girl that," and rubbed each others belly and say: "Look at how this," and "Look at how that." I was getting tired of the shit. Blee knew he made a big ass mistake with this.
 Damn, I had to move in with Steph. Every night I had to be home at seven or

Me Tears

so. No matter what. She was getting me sick with all of the vitamins, and doctor visits, and couldn't cook worth a damn. "Am I getting big?" she would ask. She was always fixing all types of vegetables and stuff. The fish was all she had going for her, she fucked up everything else. I couldn't eat certain foods because my sperm wouldn't be right or something. I couldn't have a beer or anything because my sperm wouldn't be healthy, wouldn't find the egg, or would be too tired when it got to the egg. You name it, I heard it. Sex was no fun now. I had to drink a certain amount of water and juice. "The doctor said," she would say.

Then, she came up with the crazy shit. I didn't read the shit she had. All the time she was in a book or magazine. After eight days the stupid chick made me put my hands behind my back and cuffed me. She said she had to get my boys excited. Something like pulling a rubber band back and then letting it go.

My torment began after she made me take these cold ass baths. She said it tightened my balls, and cause my sperm to organize, like an army. I couldn't figure how someone who had no balls could tell

Me Tears

some one with balls, how to handle balls. The bitch had balls.

After the cold water torture. I had to drink carrot juice, but that was after my having to do 100 sit- ups and a hundred push ups. The only part I liked was when she rubbed my body down with oil. I couldn't enjoy it because I was cuffed and my ankles were tied. Worst, was her jumping on my back and spanking me. I knew then, she was a freak of sorts. She never acted like this before. She would rub me over and over, and up and down and then sit on the chair with her legs open, rubbing herself. I guess that made me a freak too. She didn't have a gun to my head.

"You want some," she'd say. I did, but I couldn't get up and even when I managed to my feet she'd say "Bad boy," and push me back down. I Married a nut. But, then after I was watching for a while she would lay next to me and remove the cuffs from me. I didn't like the process but I must admit. It worked. I just wanted to give it to her. I never lasted more than a couple of minutes on those days. I use to last much longer. Steph said that it was the elastic band technique.

Me Tears

The worst part was, I could only get one shot at it a day. What's more is, she got pregnant only eight days into this thing. From the start, until her pregnancy was only about three weeks. I couldn't believe that one morning she said. "I think you did it, I'm pregnant," she didn't use a test or doctor. She just knew. I didn't want to know what Tray wanted. My life wasn't my life ever since Blee got Queen pregnant.
"You have to go now," she said.
   "Now, now?"
"Go, hurry. He said now."

Me Tears

Tray and Ragga Explaining The Organization To Us

    Then Tray reached in his drawer and pulled out his heat. Neither of us saw him with his heat before. The way he grasped the barrel was as if he missed it. Rubbing the sides of it, he smoothly placed it to the desk top.
  "See this?" not looking for a response as he kept talking, admiring his steal, a 357 magnum. He was in a trance. He looked as if he was in his past, his mind began to wonder.
  "I ain't use this since....since...shit, I don't even know when. Ain't even have to raise my voice to no one since.....since...shit, even I can't remember," he lapsed. I was thinking: "Now I know why this muthafucka don't talk. He can't talk."
    The room was filling with smoke during this conference or whatever. They smoked, we didn't. They passed the smoke back and forth not even thinking about us. Not even realizing we were at least I was getting pissed-the-fuck-off.

Me Tears

"Let me say this, and I quit with it. Who the fuck Y'all down with? You down with You: 'cause y'alls tight as fuck. I watch ya(pointing just under his left eye). Or, Y'all down w'it this shit here?" (Pointing his finger to his chest, and then slamming his fist to Ragga's chest. It was enough for the average nigga to get heated. But, Ragga seemed to get strong from that shit, a bit tougher if that were at all possible. The glare in Ragga's eyes became more intense, wanting a answer. Ragga didn't budge, it was like he didn't feel the blow, I did. You couldn't see his eyes for the redness, but his eyebrows said it all.

"Shit, I'm down with y'all man. Why you ask?" You know where we stand. What's Up?" Blee inquired.
"Nawh Black. Just for when I have to take a nigga out I have to ask. 'Cause you down one hundred percent or you down in the ground one hundred percent. I don't wound muthafuckas."

"Word," Blee understood and they knew we both understood.
"Ain't no in between shit here. We love you or not. Y'all niggas could be family now."
"Yo, no disrespect, but we Rawga now,

Me Tears

right?"

"Baby Rawga," Ragga said.

"Can we get baby weeded?" Everyone laughed.

"Yeah nigga- man, Y'all go 'head outside and smoke yo' shit. We done here."

"Don't get the fuck'n big head. Listen to them women and you'll be straight. They know the way. All you have to do is follow their lead. Personally, I didn't want to have this conversation. But hey, I do whateva because they do whatever for me. They need this shit or something. They want us to welcome y'all to the family. Me, I didn't give a fuck. They give a fuck(reaching his hands out). So, I give a fuck(slapping his hands to his chest reclining)."

"So when they don't give a fuck, you don't?" looking at Ragga.

"Now, now see," Tray sat back up, looking over to Ragga.

"That's why Steph feeling you dawg, you smart. He smart too. That's why Queen love yo' ass (pointing at Blee), 'cause you already knew without asking, you just knew. Right?"

Me Tears

"Word," Blee nodded.
"Here," Tray reached in his drawer, putting back his reach. Pulling out a bag of some of his own stash, and a few dutch.

"Y'all nigs go beam up. No cars or no shit like that though. No posting up or no shit like that neither. Don't bring too much attention to yourselves. Got it?"

"O-fucking-K," Ragga added, making his now red eyes twice as big, they were still closed looking, as his forehead stretched and his eyes stayed fixed on small. Then he smiled really big, shining his grill. You could see the entire RAWGA. Only this was a smile for real. He also had a smile that meant other shit.

"Don't smoke that shit," Tray said, as we looked at him. Not saying a word. Spit was in my mouth as if I was about to eat for the joint.

"Y'all niggas take us to the crib, then y'all can chill at the spot a minute. I'll send your wives down," Tray said with laughter.

"Yeah, Y'alls wives," they laughed together until they were almost in tears, and coughing. We could only laugh and look at each other.

"You know this is some sentimental shit. My BabyGirl and Queen getting married

Me Tears

and shit. I guess miracles do happen. Miracles do happen. Damn," shaking his head, busting out in laughter. "Y'all niggas got some shit on your hands."

"Hold up, hold up," Ragga got up and reached in the cabinet.
"This is cause for a celebration. Y'alls is partners in business and family now. We gots to drink to that shit," As he took a swallow and passed the bottle to Tray, who took a couple of swallows and past it back to Ragga, who took a swallow, a double up swallow. He looked at the bottle, mumbling, as though speaking to himself at the bottle. He trusted the bottle more than us.
"Damn," he whispered.

"Let me hold you like that baby," he said looking at the bottle and kissing it before taking another gulp, as Tray laughed and slapped the desk.

Blee reached for the bottle. Tray stopped laughing and looked at Ragga. Then, they both started to laugh.

"What the fuck with these niggas?" We just looked at each other.

"Didn't I just say that they 'pose to go to the spot after they take us home?" He looked at Ragga, who nodded and hunched

Me Tears

his shoulders.

"They must of been smoking or someth'in," both started to laugh until they bent over in the chairs, slapping the desk.

"I thought we were smoking. Maybe we should let them smoke, and then that way we could get high like them, damn," as both of us smiled. Reaching forth the bottle Ragga pulled it back.
"Fake," pulling his lids from the eye lids, upward. Holding it like that, he looked at Tray and they both busted out laughing again. Both of us started to laugh as well.
"Let's get the fuck out of here. Y'all can't smoke. Be the watch eye." Ragga laughed and let out a deep breath, laughing on the inhale.

Walking towards the door, as we got up, he grabbed both of us from under the cheek like we were his children, an looked us both in the eyes.
"We family now. Family die together. Remember that. We may not smoke together......," Tray laughed. Looking into his eyes I could tell he never said 'family' too much. I knew the words "I love you" was an impossibility for a cat like Ragga. Then, just as quickly Tray gave us hugs. The slapping the back kind of hugs. The

Me Tears

kind of hug with love that meant: "If you fuck up, You dead" kind of hug. The Mafia kiss on the cheek type of hug....Almost.

In The Office Still

We almost made it out of the office. "This 'bout lovin' a nigga. This be 'bout respecting a nigga" pointing at the desk with all four fingers and thumb pounding, no palm.
"This 'bout lovin' your ass enough to put you out of your damn misery. 'Cause you is one miserable bitch if you cross this." Drawing an imaginary line across his desk.
Ragga and Tray had a huge dark cherry looking desk, about three times larger than a normal desk. The kind you see in a bank or something. It had two big office chairs, at the same desk. They were like twins. The two computers were primarily for video games and music. They had cartridges stacked by the mile, it seemed. They were smart. Most records were in the brain.
"Let me say....Let me say this shit. We

Me Tears

paid for all this shit. You niggas stepped into this shit."

"Word," Tray added.

"You niggas respect this shit," pointing the same pointing finger at each of us.

"We tell y'all what the fuck respect is or ain't not," Tray said.

"Word," Blee agreed.

"Word," I said.

"Word," Ragga confirmed with a nod.

"That's what the fuck," Tray said.

"Harmony means niggas on the same muthafuckin' page and shit. Nigga reading this shit(pointing at one spot then another). Another nigga in the back of the newspaper. Another nigga at the beginning of a book. Another nigga watching fucking cartoons and shit. That gets muthafuckas hurt and shit," rolling his eyes in disgust. Then, just as quick his voice mumbled and you can tell he was reminiscing about something that happened. His eyes went blank, but it was no time to inject anything. He was in a different world, and then he came back.

"Harmony," his voice raised up and he hit the desk, as if lack of harmony did some shit in his life.

Me Tears

"Harmony," both of us repeated. I didn't know what to think. Tray was watching our eyes. Ragga's veins began to pulse in his temples and he tightened his jaws. It must have been a conversation they had in their past about 'harmony' or something. It was as if he was smoking something other than weed. He reminded me of when Blee, when he spoke of popping niggas.

"Yeah," Blee said. The two of them were vibing.

"Sometimes you never know. But, one thing fo'sho' is a dead nigga is one better than one you don't know 'bout. It's like a brother dancing to rock, while the beat is Hip-Hop."

"Fuck not knowing, " I added.

"Word," Tray said. Ragga had come back all the way by now. He looked calm, realizing he was cought in some shit.

"See this nigga right here?" Pointing a Ragga. "Shit ain't right, nigga don't sleep. I seen the nigga stay up for days 'cause he thought if he went to bed, it would be him asleep forever. Just like the nigga he had to make sleep forever."

"Yeah, yeah," Blee got excited as if a light went off in his head. It was like Tray was reading his mind. Ragga looked at

Me Tears

Blee and nodded.

"My heart rate stays up until shit is normal. Normal is that out of beat nigga not moving." Ragga said.

"Word. Like a niggas not right or something. I hate that." To see this shit, was like Blee had found his soul mate or something. The chairs of both Ragga and Tray were as if dancing, swiveling from left to right in perfect harmony, slowly.

    I never understood the mind set of Blee. Although I understood the end results of some of his actions, after the fact. I began to think about why he never got scared. It was starting to get spooky. Just like a crook knows a crook. Blee found someone he could relate to, and from the looks of things Ragga respected Blee. I was to Blee, like Tray was to Ragga. The cooler, calmer side, so to speak. If nothing else, we developed an understanding with Tray, and Ragga. If nothing less, we were gonna be knowing more things. If nothing else we were going to be given more responsibility, and if nothing else, we knew we were dead ass muthas, if we blew it. If nothing else, I had Blee on my side. If nothing else, I knew if I fucked up, Blee would do me or Ragga would do him, if

Me Tears

need be.

"Sometimes you show respect for a brotha by putting one more in his ass.....not wanting a nigga to suffer. Not that I ever put one in a nigga. I ain't saying that. But, a gut shot or something shows no respect to a brotha, for real." Blee began to suddenly lean forward a bit more.

"What you mean?" he had to ask.

"I mean, why make a nigga suffer?"

"Yo, Yo, let me ask you some shit. 'Cause, you look like you might know this shit,"

"Nawh man, I don't want to hear no more of this bullshit man –B–word," I tried to stop him. Tray looked at me.

"Chill nigga. Go 'head with the bullshit."

"Wha, What?"

"Heaven," Blee spitted.

"What, What the fuck man?" Looking and laughing at the confusion on Tray's face. Pointing at Tray. "Exactly."

"Nawh man, heaven. Not that I sent anyone there before," Now Blee was getting into the word game with Ragga, who nodded, understanding.

"Here we go," I rolled my eyes.

"Check it," Leaning forward.

"Why do people be scared to go to

Me Tears

heaven, especially when it's good. Why they bitch out before you heat they ass? Not that I ever heated a nigga. I'm just saying. I have seen the shit. You know what I'm saying?" Looking at me, then Ragga. We knew he was talking about his own shit. Shit, I seen him do shit.

"Why niggas be scared and shit on themselves and shit, start pissing and shit? If you gonna get popped, hold your ass cheeks tight. Know what I'm saying? You going to heaven."

    They told us about a lot of shit in life. They told us about how and why they did the things they did to us as kids and all. They told us more than we needed to know about our wives as well. After this conversation, we were like Ragga and Tray's personal drivers to New York, as we went on spur of the moment trips, late at night into the city.

Me Tears

Rawga

The one reason as to why Tray never put fire to Blee was because he respected his ways, and that reminded him of himself as a youth. When he was younger Tray would do shit for the hell of it too. All the things Blee did the Stab and everyone seen "The four" heard of it. Most people would think Blee was crazy. But, to the four he was normal. How that is? Who knows? Blee told me what happened with Queen and Tray one day when they worked the block years ago, and that help put things into perspective.

Queen was out at the crib with some nigga from the crew they had back then. Tray came home and heard some fucking going on in her room. The door was said to be closed, but not locked. Tray could only see a brotha's ass was up in the air and Queen was spread the fuck out. It is said that Tray didn't say shit for a minute. Then, he pulled on that brotha. He popped a cap right in the nigga's ass. You could imagine how big his eyes must have gotten. I don't think it had anything to do

Me Tears

with being caught in the pussy. It was beyond that, especially when your ass is burning. Queen thought the nigga was coming or something. Chicks love to think their pussy is that good to make a nigga holla. That is until she saw Tray standing there and the nigga was crying and pleading.

"What the fuck you doing nigga?"

The brotha couldn't say shit for the heat, and sweat and tears. Queen jumped the fuck up butt naked and slapped Tray. "What's the fuck the matter with you?"

"What's wrong with yo' ass? Why this booty nigga in my crib?"

"I ain't never tell you who to be with."

"Look, don't have this punk muthafucka in my shit...word."

"I'll get my own then."

"Don't you....Nigga if I ever see you up in my shit again, the next one goes to the dome...word. Punk ass nigga." Tray mumbled.

"Why you did this shit Tray? This my man now. You know me and Cuz is through."

"What?"

"This my new man."

"Please Queen," as he pointed the barrel

Me Tears

at the brotha.

"This is your bitch?" The brotha didn't say shit. Tray smacked him and zipped down his pants.

"Now, you either gonna suck on this," pulling out his dick. "Or, you can suck on this," putting the heat to the side of the brotha's jaw. "Either way Ain't no blanks."

"You gonna kill a nigga? For what?" Queen said.

"Shut the fuck up. I ain't talking to you. What nigga?" Tray pointed the gun, and looked at him. The nigga dropped to his knees like a bitch and not even a second later she kicked that nigga to the jaw and started whipping his ass. Tray started to laugh at the whole situation.

"They say this nigga was a bitch for real. Put some damn clothes on," he told her.

"You got this muthafucka bleeding all over my shit. This is not a pretty sight at all. I'll bust yo' ass Queen you bring another nigga like this in my shit. Look at the muthafucka. I just bought this shit. The bitch should have a pad on. Give the bitch one of your pads. I think that shit went through his ass. Yo nigga, get your ass to the doctor, or do you want to go to the morgue? I ain't gotta say this shit

Me Tears

didn't happen here. Do I?" Tray said as he shook his head in disbelief.

"Get the fuck out, " Queen said crying.

"You gotta be stronger than that shit Queen," Tray said, giving her a fist tap to the chin. Blee said that Queen also told him that he was the only nigga Tray didn't speak on or have a problem with, when he found out she was riding the pony.

Me Tears

We Made it!!!

Both Queen and Steph had Rawga tattoos on their backs. Blee and Ragga were sitting at the table in the corner. They were two of a kind to tell you the truth.

"What Up?"

"Yo," they both said.

"What's going on at eight in the fucking morning?"

Blee smiled. "Oh, Steph's pregnant."

"Oh thanks, she just told me."

"Yeah, Queen just told me dawg...family."

"You caused enough shit in my life nigga. What the fuck you done did now?" Tray came in. Now, I knew something was up. I never seen the brother in the morning.

"Don't go getting the big head either of you." Ragga said.

"I don't wanna have to swell you nigga's for real. Y'all some brave muthafuckas cause I wouldn't be getting married or no shit myself." as Ragga flashed RAWGA, and polished his grill.

"Y'all gonna get your shits done."

Me Tears

"What shit?"

"Grills nigga...What?" Blee smiled. Then I smiled.

"This ain't my idea, word," Ragga said.

"Them wives," Tray said.

"We ain't gotta get married?"

"Oh, you getting married."

"Damn right," Ragga echoed.

"Y'all going to the doctor this morning. Go by the shop and pick out your shit." Tray pulled about ten grand from his pocket for the both of us.

"Yeah, you all know where the doctor office is," Ragga said. The dentist was gonna make us some grills, molded, for real.

I noticed Them Niggas was absent, they had grills. The Stab didn't have grills. That meant that we got bumped up over the Stab, and on par with Them Niggas.

"You don't want them shits pulled out after you get them. They don't go to the grave with yo' ass, feel me?" Tray said.

"You don't be socializing with them brothas on the crew neither. 'Bout nothing. You wanna talk, we here. You down with us that's that. You two will be spreading out about a block to the east and west of

Me Tears

the block. You pick a couple niggas and start up your own shit. No sales, just spread out. Y'all buy up a few of them cribs over there. I don't need y'all working, not ever. Queen and Steph will put y'all up on shit. They ain't working no more. See what your dicks got you?" Ragga laughed, as Tray continued.
"Y'all hear from us, and your wives that's it. Don't want no fuck ups either. I'll see y'all tonight at Steph's....One." Tray headed out the other door this time, the back way.
"Yo, we family now?" Looking at Ragga.
"Muthafuckas please. Just see this shit. Don't do your shit like my shit or I'll snatch them shits out."
"Word," Blee said.
"Word," I nodded.

Me Tears

Wednesday

The wives saw our grills on Tuesday. My face almost cracked when I saw Steph. She put her entire hands in my mouth, separating my lips just to glimpse my teeth. I decided on the white gold and diamonds with a platinum crown on the lower grill. Ragga had his on the upper and lower, and so did Tray. We did ours with crowns on the upper front two with the full bottom. "Floss for mommy," Steph said as I smiled each time. To hear her speak with Queen on the phone boosted my ego, if that were any more possible. She was proud of me, and Queen was crazy about Blee. Every other word was teeth or wedding.

The wedding was not a problem. It was going down in two weeks. It wasn't planned: family and crew only. They didn't have a group of women friends. They only knew women they were in the life with. They were on a level that most women in the 'hood didn't understand. A lot of niggas was gonna get pussy that day from all of Queen's chicks.

The funniest thing was seeing all the

Me Tears

crew in tuxedo wear. Many didn't understand ceremony. The only thing that came close was when we cracked a forty, and blessed our beloved. They didn't know where anything went. They did all have a fresh one. Them Niggas came with their family. It was the only humanity I saw in them since meeting them. They even spoke to me and Blee like they weren't ever going to kill us. They had personality, and manners.

    Then, I almost lost it when I saw Tray and Ragga with their wives or women and not the "Other Side" chicks. They had babies too, and the babies called Queen and Steph "Auntie". You wouldn't think that we were a bunch of 'hood cats to look at us, except when we flossed.

    Hell, after the wedding things changed even more. Tray and Ragga disappeared almost completely. The crew on the blocks didn't really know who they were, especially newer cats. We expanded to more streets outside of our base. Let's face it, that entire side of town was ours.

    Now, all the problems and concerns came to me an Blee, and we shared them with the wives who gave us advice. That advice came from Tray and Ragga. We

Me Tears

weren't like baby Tray and baby Ragga to the fellas on the block. The Stab reported to us, but didn't too much appreciate us. The green eyed devil is always around, especially in the business. The good thing is, we could spit at Tray and Ragga at will. The only thing about that was the wives spitted at us. They brought us word from the Boss and not only that, we were their men. All we heard was mouth, both business and family shit.

    I understood what was going on to a point. Tray and Ragga and Them Niggas were always taking vacations, and plotting things. Sometimes with or without their family. All of their wives had professional jobs. Queen and Steph was always out at our real homes with the babies. We could only go home with them when The Stab was in full force. We could only go home escorted by Clive, and Martini. They called him Martini because he was only five feet or so. He was the shortest of Them Niggas.

    When ever they picked us up, they had dough. They didn't give that shit to us. They gave it to the women. We didn't know by who or how the stash got to Ragga, it just did. Blee and I could not smoke that much. We had to be on point.   We did our

Me Tears

smoking on Sundays and Mondays. We had to be different from the crew, they smoked at will. The only fear I had, was another baby.

Stacy, and her other child

It was about this time that another one of the things caused by Dez happened. Stacy was in torment over their last child together. The child was only twelve. She had developed this cough.

She never told anyone that she felt sick or anything. They thought that she was susceptible to colds and everything. That is until she came down with pneumonia. She stayed in the hospital for a while until they finally ran tests on her. Come to find out

Me Tears

she was sleeping with this fourteen year old cat in our crew who had some how caught the chicken. She died a month or so later with complications brought on by AIDS.

Stacy didn't know how to feel. She totally distanced herself from everyone. She trusted no one.

Mama Auntie

Mama Auntie, Steph and Queen's grandmother waited until Thanksgiving. Her daughter had since died of unknown causes. She knew all along that this was going to be the day. She had enough of the evil from the past. She greeted everyone at the door with a loving hug and several kisses. Even the babies she watched and looked over. Just as ducks in a row, only this day she was to be the wolf.

Me Tears

Queen and Blee were first over. It was to be a sort of putting the family back together event. I had to handle the block. It was Thanksgiving, that's dough day. They came with their child, Baby Blee in tow. He was but three at best. With another only three months in the future. "The Life' was away from them now.

Blee had decided to give it up. He wore simple clothes now. Since Tray and Ragga were gone, the block was left to Them Niggas and others. You couldn't recognize him with the regular clothes and haircut. He had no flash, but in his mouth. He only sat around all day and cut hair at the shop, and was a husband. The wives still didn't know the truth.

Mama Auntie knew what was going on. She and the wise women were hatching up schemes and such ever since. It was her day to deal the cards which would be played, jokers them all.

Steph then came with her baby. The little rose we called her. It was all that remained of the former life she had. Things were stressed as Tray and Ragga disappeared. Since the hustling was over, we decided to get a divorce if things didn't get better between us.

Me Tears

Steph and Queen tolerated each other, but had long lost respect for each other. Queen didn't know that Slim told Blee that it was her plot that killed Cuz, Blee's brother. It was Queen's betrayal that helped turn Steph from a bright eyed level headed woman, into one much as Queen's mother in their past days. Steph had to have a drink or smoke constantly. Queen took away from Steph more than Steph could handle.

Steph could care less about appearances anymore. Just as her mother's sister slept with her mother's husband. The two sisters' relationship turned on the same thing. Steph had lost everyone. She was Mama Auntie's favorite.

"Go lay down child. You feel better later, rest yourself. I'll take the baby."
"You sure mama?"
"BabyGirl go on," Steph didn't want the company of Queen and them anyhow. She totally changed just as Stacey had after finding out about Cuz, Blee and Queen.

Although Steph was on the couch, her son came in to watch television. It was pretty much the end for Blee, Queen and their baby. It was all he could do with Mama Auntie's back turned at the stove, as it hissed of gas.

Me Tears

He could feel the grog overcoming him as his eyes began to lose focus. He reached for what would be the last time, firing off two shots as he slumped over the table from the poison Mama Auntie had put in drinks they were given. One shot hitting Mama in the back, the other hitting the stove, causing the explosion in the kitchen.

She fell onto the stove and then her entire head snapped back as she was on fire and lying on the floor from the explosion. The flash of fire came pass them at the table, as Blee was leaning to the floor. No one could move from the poison they had been given. Only their eyes had movement, and the breathing was faint at best. The fire began to consume the kitchen as Steph was crawling on the floor with the baby towards the front door, pass the dining room table.

Queen was holding on with tears to her eyes but couldn't move gasping for air, as Mama Auntie was rolling from side to side on the floor, on fire, kicking. She was kicking her last kicks, trembling and uselessly waving her arms which were flamed in fire. The bullet in her back was the least of her worries.

Coughing and pushing her son out of the front door, Steph reached back, after

Me Tears

looking back. Looking at Queen who's head was facing her, with eyes open not able to move because of the poison. Blee couldn't move neither as he was on the floor, as Queen had tears in her eyes, as her mouth tried to open.   Steph managed to reach back to Blee and snatch his collar, as Queens hair began to smoke, sizzle and then catch fire. The water from Queen's eyes wasn't enough to help her situation. With all of her strength, Steph couldn't move Blee. So, she fell backwards holding on to him, managing to pull him across the threshold.

   Then crawling back , she grabbed their baby, looking up at Queen looking at her. It was too late, as the hair on her head caught full of fire, and the oils popped and fried. Steph with tears in her eyes swallowed, as Queen's mouth opened and she became inflamed, as her tears were no match for the fire. Steph could have helped Queen by just putting one in her from the gun that was on the floor. Instead, she watched her involuntarily twitch from the fire.

   "Run baby, go to the sidewalk," Steph yelled to her child from the steps.

   Although being dragged Blee grunted and grunted. Queen was still moving, watching and coughing, convulsing, looking

Me Tears

helplessly as the fire got hotter on her. Steph left Blee hanging at the top of the stairs as she knelt and got the other child out and down the steps. No sooner had she reached the bottom step, Blee came tumbling down with his leg on fire. Then, a second explosion came, and along came the fire trucks and such.

    The trucks couldn't save those left behind. No one knew that Auntie died from a gunshot wound. Steph, the professional she was, didn't forget to grab that gun. She was now the Queen. The final reports stated the same thing. They said the deaths were from smoke inhalation. They missed the poison and the bullets. They never did an autopsy. The bodies were burned too badly. Since it was an explosion in the kitchen, they let the fire burn the house completely. Steph, Blee and the baby made it out of the house okay. Blee's son didn't make it. He died on the way to the hospital.

    Blee was on the stretcher when he got the cold chill. With the mask to his face, he glanced someone standing across the street with this huge hat and a lot of hair, leaning on a staff with beads on it, Just watching. Steph looked over and saw the same person. It was the person outside of the window

Me Tears

when her little brother passed away years earlier. Blee didn't think Mama Auntie was his enemy. She told him that Cuz was his brother, and that Dez was his father. She just didn't tell him about the curse, as she used him to kill Tray and Ragga.

    Them Niggas didn't know much except that they were all Dez's children. They wouldn't kill any of them. That's why one of us had to be the one responsible. We were still the ones as far as they were concerned.

Me Tears

The End-Continued From the Beginning

"You see, we figured this shit out. One of you or both of you. It don't matter to us which one of you know where the fuck the money is. We know what they had that day, and we know you niggas did them." Martini said.

"What Dough?" I answered.

"The Dough, that's what dough."

"We ain't got shit." Blee laughs.

"Is that what this is about?"

"You got dough?" Blee looked at me.

"Stop the bullshit man."

"Nigga let me tell you niggas something."

"Not this shit. Please- don't man."

"If you cats gonna pop me, pop me for some shit I did." Blee said.

"I ain't do shit." I made sure they heard.

"Mafuckas dying and you two seem to be the only niggas around."

"Mafuckas die when y'all ass around. We ain't think 'bout putt'in no shit to your head."

"Yeah, and you got some nerves for some nigga 'bout to die."

Me Tears

"Yeah, we got balls, but no cash."

"I'm confessing," I looked at Blee wondering what he was talking about. "I did them muthafuckas, but I ain't got no cash. Now, that's the truth, pull the mafucka trigga and let me go to heaven. I am sorry for all the wrong I did." Blee raised his hands to the sky.

"This is not the time for this stupid shit Blee."

"You betta confess too man. Remember heaven man. Fuck these niggas man."

"What's he talking about?" One of Them Niggas asked.

"This nigga........He obsessed with death and heaven.......I don't know."

"Confess some shit." The nigga put the gun to my temple. I looked at Blee.

"Go 'head nigga." He grilled me, breathing hard.

"This shit better be good too." Martini said.

"I shot Cuz with Queen. Queen shot the nigga. I was there. Things were all set in place. Only I had no idea of what was going on," recounting what happened that day. Three out of four didn't seem that bad. Finding out that they rolled like that was a surprise. Including me in this scheme didn't

Me Tears

set well.

"Take me to the club." Queen stated.

"What club?"

"On the east side."

"East side?" That's were a totally different crew worked. That's where Cuz was, and where Cuz was, is where trouble was.

"I know you ain't....."

"Just drive the fucking car behind my damn car." Queen was pissed. She made no bones about it. The rolling of her eyes and floss' she represented that day. Those extra fitted jeans, and nails with the Clark sandals set the outfit right. She wasn't dressed up so to speak, just put together to drop dead a brotha. She was dressed like she wanted some dick.

When we got to the club it wasn't long after that Cuz came out with Queen. Then, my phone rang, it was Tray. The strange shit was, he never called me directly like this.

"You do what the fuck you suppose to nigga." He said.

Not a minute later, we were on the road to I have no idea. Then, Queen stopped the car, and got out, coming around to my driver side.

Me Tears

"Here," she gave me a key to a motel room. "What's this?'
"When the nigga come, you do what you gotta do."

    Cuz had gone back inside the bar. Queen had told him when and where to come, so they could patch shit up. Me, I was the nigga that was suppose to do him. It wasn't only me. Not even an hour had past and there was a knock at the door. It was Queen, standing behind Cuz, and then a push, as Cuz went to the bed.

"Go 'head nigga," ZIP, ZIP. To the brain and the chest. It was over that quick. Queen stood their looking at the nigga, or once nigga.

    Cuz rolled onto the floor. What am I saying? He didn't roll, when you have a choice you may roll. He fell to the floor. I guess they found him.

    I heard through the streets he had gotten popped. The only one in the family upset was Steph. It was her cousin. Blee jumped for joy, and thought the shit should have happened sooner. Steph didn't appreciate Queen after that. What got to me, was what Queen did after the nigga rolled, or fell to the floor.

Me Tears

"Shit, we know that shit." One of Them Niggas said.

"Shit, I know that nigga," Blee said, not helping the situation.

"She was crazy Blee. You should have never messed with that chick."

"What the fuck you talking about?"

"Yo, after the nigga was on the floor and shit, she put the gun to my head." looking at Blee.

"You here nigga." Blee was grill'in me.

"That's because she made me nigga."

"Made you?"

"She pointed the gun to my head and told me to rub her breasts and shit." Blee was looking like 'what'. Then she said: "Pull my pants down nigga and take your time. Get the fuck on your knees. You know me. You won't eat pussy. You don't eat pussy. You pull that shit with my sister. She might go for that shit," she said.

"Then she brought my head between her legs and told me to lick." Looking at Blee. "You know I ain't with that shit."

"Then what? You fucked her?" Blee asked.

"Mafucka, she just smoked one nigga. She pulled me up to her. I wasn't even hard nigga. What the hell you want me to do. I

Me Tears

couldn't put it inside her. She was getting off on that shit, and she began to get off with that shit." I continued the story.

"Look at your dead ass," she was looking at Cuz on the floor.
She then got up on her hands and knees, and said
"Put it in from behind. Yeah, let me look at this stupid muthafucka," she said, looking at Cuz dead ass on the floor.
"Word- man, She just started to back up like crazy on me. The shit was strange as fuck. Then, she unbuttoned that dead mafuckas pants, and started to feel up on his shit." Then she said:
"Nawh, this shit ain't what it use to be," as she laughed.
"Then she grabbed my dick and put it in her mouth."
"That's better, that's what the fuck I'm talking about," she said.
"I thought it was some spooky type shit. Then, she tells me two months later that the baby that she was carrying was mine. I told Steph about all this shit, and she explained shit to me about how Dez raped Queen and that the baby she had was put up for

Me Tears

adoption. She also said that Cuz found out while he was in jail, and didn't want her anymore. That's why she acted like she did. I guess that that's why Steph picked you out of the fire and not her. For one, she said she was setting Queen out of her misery. Two, she knew you were Dez's child and Cuz's half brother. I didn't find none of this shit out until after Cuz was done....Word."

The room was quiet and Blee just looked at me. Them Niggas were in shock.

"That's good. Damn," one of them said, and another agreed.

"If you don't top that. I doubt if you could," as he pointed the heat at Blee. "Don't man, don't do it Blee." I knew what he was gonna say.

"Why nigga?"

"This ain't no time for that shit Blee."

"Don't and that's the last thing you don't say." One said.

"I should have popped your ass." Blee said.

"If you would have done me nigga, It would have been your ass in that burnt up house,word."

"He got a point." One of Them Niggas

Me Tears

said.

"I guess," Blee turned away.

"You spit some shit better than that shit this nigga over here said," pointing at me.

"Shit, I will let you both go." Martini said.

"Word?" Blee looked at me.

"No man!" The thirty eight cocked at my head.

"Tell that nigga," I changed my mind.

"Nawh, you tell them for me. I don't really give a fuck." Blee sucked his teeth.

"Someone better." Martini commanded.

"It was the same thing as before. The four of us went to New York to cop. They must have gotten at least ten cakes this time. We didn't role that deep. Sometimes, if too many niggas go, they say it makes other niggas nervous. That's what they told us when we wondered about not having You Niggas with us.

Shit was smooth and we hauled ass out of the city. When we got on the highway, out of nowhere man: "Blow! Blow!Blow!Blow!"

POP-POP-POP-POP-POP-POP-POP. I have no idea how many I heard. It was all I could do to keep the car straight and on the

Me Tears

road. The shit didn't look pretty at all. I wish that I could actually have not looked, but to see that shit, you find yourself not being able to look away. You catch yourself wondering {damn}. Before I could get out a word.

"Don't think I don't know nigga."

"Yo Blee-man."

"Yeah, I know you killed my brother."

"What the fuck you smoking nigga." I couldn't think straight because the way Tray and Ragga looked in the back seat.

"Oh, don't worry 'bout them muthafuckas."

"What the fuck is going on nigga?"

"Cuz, that nigga was my brother, man."

"What?"

"Shit yeah."

"You didn't say no shit 'bout that."

"Chill yo, I know you didn't know. Shit, I didn't know until recently."

"Yo, I ain't know man."

"Them muthafuckas knew. What? I was next."

"Yo, I don't know 'bout that type shit. You know that. I did just what I was told."

"Well you won't have to worry 'bout them coming up with no more bright ideas now," pointing the gun at them dead bodies in the

Me Tears

back seat.
 "Guess not."
"Y'all niggas got something to say?' looking back at his work in the back seat.
"See, I couldn't forgive no shit like that. Them muthafuckas was brothers, they killed my brother. They thought that we were gonna try to take over."
 "Was you?"
"How the fuck should I know. I ain't know this shit 'til the nigga was dead. Shit, I don't know if Cuz knew or not. Shit, I was humping my own brother's ex nigga. Married to the bitch now. She knows."
 "Come on, word?"
"Who went with your ass to set him up?"
 "Word, you right."
"The only one who probably didn't have anything to do with this shit is Steph."
 "Then, you fucking my wife?"
"What?"
 "She told me she had to give you a piece of ass just to keep you quiet nigga."
"Don't say that shit man. It wasn't like that."
 "Oh, don't worry, when I told Steph, she gave me some too. I ain't mad at your ass nigga. Just kidding. This was your

Me Tears

muthafucking idea to do this shit.: "Claim the baby! Remember nigga?"

"You know you ain't had no choice."

"Well, I got choices now muthafucka, because them muthafuckas ain't got nothing to say no damn more. See, this is some prophetic type shit. I told you when we were kids. I killed them mafuckas......Remember?"

"What the fuck now?"

"We got to get rid of these niggas."

"How you gonna manage that shit."

"Why the fuck you think I built that big ass barbeque pit in the backyard?"

"I thought you were going to do a cow or something on that shit."

"Nawh nigga, we rap these niggas up, cut and burn they ass."

"That's what all the wood and shit is for?"

"Exactly nigga."

"How you gonna explain that shit, these niggas missing?"

"Like on that 'Mysteries' shit from TV."

"What?"

"They told our ass to sit in the car a block behind them when they made the buy nigga. Then all of a sudden niggas came up, got in the car and that's the last we seen them.

Me Tears

We tried to follow them. Remember?" He started to paint a picture.

"Yeah, Yeah we lost them in traffic."

"We ain't know the Bronx and shit like that, so we hauled ass."

"I'm getting a divorce."

"Nawh man."

"Nawh man? What the fuck you talking about."

"Yo man! Don't make no sudden moves like that cousin. You got to stay put and cool."

"Shit, what the use of us being married, fucking each other wives and shit?

"They don't know we know. Them bitches is crazy, and as long as they don't know we know, fuck it."

{Queen was at my house with Steph when we got in that night. Blee had everything all figured out. The pit was in the back and we turned the lights off and drove right to the pit, and took them from the back seat. Blee had about twenty gallons of gasoline he stored in the garage, along with the wood and charcoal. He put the wood and charcoals at the bottom and lit them and then put them on top, right on the grill. I knew I'd never eat anything off of

Me Tears

this grill. Then, he started to douse them with gas, as the flames shot up at least ten feet in the air. Over and over he did this. Then, the coals got hot, and they began to burn, as the smell was too much. Even smoking weed didn't help. He covered them, just like they were roasters, with the metal flap and then we started to spray down the car, and clean it. Thank goodness, they were chest and forehead shots. Blee didn't make much of a mess. But now I realize why Queen was keeping Steph preoccupied. On a couple of occasions I wondered how it was she never heard us outside......although she peeked out the window a few times.}

"What we gonna do with the shit?"
 "Put that shit away."
"Where?"
 "It don't matter. Bury it or something. We might need that shit to start our own shit up one day."
"Let's plant that shit behind the pit."
   They were cooking for about two hours now, when Blee opened the lid again. He kept the wood heavy underneath, and the gas pouring on top. It was like he did this before. It wasn't long after Queen came

Me Tears

home and we were almost finished. Blee went in the house with her and I stayed in the yard. I had to get them grills and shit like that. After about five hours there were nothing but ashes.

"Shit, were them brothas your brothers? You popped your own brothers?" One of Them Niggas asked.

I could only look and shake my head, and hunch my shoulders. Then Steph and Ray came through the door. They must have been listening to the entire thing from the other room.

- - - - -'POP-POP'   BabyGirl put two shots in Blee, while Ray added a few more-"Blow, Blow, Blow." I jumped the fuck up.

"Where the fuck you going?" Ray asked, as Steph looked over at me, as her hand rested to her side.

"No where. Heaven, Hell, I don't know."

"Yeah, I was listening to that shit." Steph said. "It was pretty much what you told me before," Steph finished.

"Yo, I just told shit like it was." I looked around.

"Ya'll know what the fuck I did and didn't do."

"Where the shit?'

Me Tears

"What shit?"

"Oh, this Jeopardy or Wheel of Fortune or some shit nigga? You don't get another guess or spin at the mafuck'in wheel."

"Probably still the fuck out there. I ain't go back. What the hell is going on?"

"They wasn't gonna kill that nigga (referring to Blee). They knew Blee and Cuz where half brothers and shit. Cuz was gonna take Tray and Ragga out. So, they took him out." Ray stated, finally lowering his joint.

"You all don' t know the half of shit. We were in the blocks. Dez and Cuz was making plans all along. Cuz had promised Dez that he would get him out. Dez thought that Tray and Ragga wanted shit to themselves. That was far from the truth." He continued as he sat.

"They were in the commons room up in the block. All the other brothas stayed in their cells that morning. Dez wanted to speak to Cuz alone. I heard them cats from my cell. Dez told Cuz that the only way that he could ever be anything on the block was to take what he wanted. That meant even if he had to go through Ragga and Tray. He was the one that pumped him up to do all that shit when he got out. Tray and Ragga

Me Tears

knew that Cuz was gonna start some shit. Dez came from a time and place where all that happened was shit like that, brotha killing brotha.

    There was never any peace in the muthafucka's life. If shit was going well, it wasn't right with Dez. I knew them cats, Tray and Ragga. They did the best for all of us, like a family should be. I would have tried to convince them otherwise, but they would have dead my ass. Blee may have been the one to pop the bossmen, and Cuz may have been hit by your ass, and Queen, but the shit went deeper. This shit came over from the islands with that nigga Dez.

    You can't do the shit he did and not pay for it. Hell, all the shit he did, his soul wasn't enough to pay for all the chaos and lives he altered. Shit like that gets passed on to your seed. Even though Tray and Ragga were real brothas, them spirits in Jamaica don't want to know that type shit. Sometimes it's an eye for an eye regardless if you believe in the New Testament or not. That just happens to be your reality. You can't do what the fuck you want in this life and think that just because you have dough or cross a fucking ocean that you reached home plate or no shit like that."

Me Tears

"Using my ass, and y'all got me the fuck in here on my knees for what?" Interrupting Ray, and looking at Steph.

"Please man, Cuz and Blee couldn't do but one thing and that was try to take over shit. If he knew Cuz was his brother first, shit would had been worst with both them mafuckas alive at the end, and at the same time."

"What about Queen?"

"Queen wanted to be the Queen. It didn't matter with who." Steph said.

"Now what?" It was better than shoot me.

"We hold this shit down. Me and you. We always held this shit down together," pointing at Them Niggas and Ray. Unless you still want that Sheila bitch. Hey, Tray and them ain't here now. You make up your own mind. I ain't mad at cha'."

Me Tears

BabyGirl

    The Cypress trees and la la land left my ass. Them Niggas and Ray rapped that dead nigga up and hauled him away to somewhere. Rather than kneel, I sat and looked up at BabyGirl.
  "What you gonna do?" She asked.
"I'm going the fuck home and fry me some mafuckin' chicken and fries."
  "You crazy Slim," as she chuckled and shook her head, unloading and checking her clip and snapping it back for the ready...
"Nawh, I ain't crazy. Umma do some regular people shit, unless you gonna pop my ass. I don't know."
  "What about the dough?"
"Fuck the dough and the 'caine."
  "You mean, you know where the shit is? You know where the 'caine is too?
"Shit yeah."
  "You was gonna die over that shit?"
"Fuck that shit. We got seed together. Wanna make a baby? Um' down with that shit."
  "You silly," as she began to laugh.

Me Tears

"Hell, I'm getting me a regular people type job and raise me some regular type babies. Now, if you want to go on with your life like it is-----I ain't mad at cha'-word."

"What? Fuck the money and shit?"

"Look—, I made up my mind on the ground a few minutes ago," as I stood.

"And—?

"Death or regular people shit, if God brought me through this shit," seriously looking at BabyGirl. "I'm tired of shit like bitches fucking me next to dead niggas, and with guns to my head and all that eating shit. I'm going home and gonna eat some regular fuckin' food and we gonna do some regular type fuckin' and this nigga wanna make a regular type baby if that's alright with you BabyGirl, or I'll go and find someone down with me like that. No, No, fuck that. I am having intercourse. That means, scripted like, book type shit. No whips, chains, or tying a nigga up or none of that bullshit. I need a chick on her damn back, with her legs the fuck open and her mouth shut-the-fuck-up.—word."

"How 'bout when you done? Then, I can take over? You know your ass gonna be done."

"Maybe after.....-Hands that's it."

Me Tears

"That's it?"

"Yeah. Then, I want some Luther Vandross, Anita Baker type love happening tunes playing. Like, like, "I Apologize," and "Make Me A Believer," and things like that."

"Nothing else? No mouth?"

"Just at the beginning—You know," as we smiled.

"Sheila..... What about her?"

"Sheila what? How the fuck she get here?" drawing an imaginary circle, and patting his chest.

"You want regular shit with her?"

"Whomever giving me regular type shit."

"I'll kill that bitch."

"Come on now. Take that shit down BabyGirl."

"I don't want to hear no shit about she had no fuckin' gun to your head and shit. Umma take her ass out before all that shit even get a chance to happen. I slept on Queen. Shit nigga, if you gonna do some shit with someone other than me...............Shit, you owe me one. How the fuck can someone get something from you that I never got and I'm your mafuck'in wife and shit."

"What the fuck you sayin'?"

" What I'm saying is........If the bitch ends up

Me Tears

missing don't come asking me shit."
"Cut the shit."
 "If you love that chick, you betta start doing the damn thing, because I ain't gonna be looking in her mug wondering if she's getting from you what I'm lacking."
"Yeah, then if I do 'The Damn Thing', you gonna say I love her.
 "Nawh, I can live with just that."

Me Tears

Peace On Earth

Peace is a symbol, a symbol of love.
All of it comes from happiness above.
We all share peace with our minds and hearts.
Peace does not come from cherries and tarts.
We all have to love plus cherish it dear.
We just cannot wait for loving next year.

If we'll stand together from our very birth,
We'll become one and have PEACE ON EARTH.

By: Twoniesha L. Moore
Victory Middle School-Portland Oregon

Starry Sky

He says he loves the way I walk
But, he's speechless when we talk.

He says he loves my almond shape eyes
But together, we are never the moon nor the stars in the starry skies.

One of these days I will pack and go
But the money is so good how can I go?

When we were first brought together I thought the love was forever.
I didn't marry him for the money or the treasures.
I married him to escape the moments and the unpleasant pleasures.
But I find myself once again trapped like a soda bottle, opened and recapped.

They only use me to mesmerize their fantasies,
But believe me love isn't what it always seems.
The way I walked was loveless

My talking became speechless
My almonds became dreary eyes

And I soon after joined the moon
and the stars in the starry skies.

By: Emily McClary
    Kingstree, South Carolina

Me Tears

A sneak previews of my future releases. I didn't include Mr. Biggs Women because of the adult content. For anyone interested in keeping up with my writings please use my email address and I will be more than glad to place you on the email list, and you will get it first. Thanks, peace and I hope to see you at Karibu..

"And 'G' Is For"

   Goodguggaleemook is all I can say. That's all I know when she walks into the room. Just like Grady I lose all sense of mind and began to slur and drool as I see those hips do there hip thing, and her ass does the ass thing as if they were doing it apart.
   I know that sooner or later my toes will curl, just don't know when. She knows exactly what she's doing. Why would she put on those shoes, especially when she isn't going anywhere tonight. Leaving me sitting in the living room watching television. She knows I cut my eyes with each passing. It's not as if she needed the make-up. We aren't going anywhere. Still she goes through it.
   The skirt, and the see through top that I wondered about her buying. I thought she was going to wear it to work or something. Silly me, I thought she bought it for the next guy. Silly me.
"You ready?" She asked.
 "Where are we going?"
"I figured out to the movies or something."
"Damn." I thought to myself. I thought it was my time.
   Now I have to protect what is mine. I can't let her go out looking like that without me. That would be my fault, her not coming home. The next man would go.
   It wasn't long before we made it to the movies and she held my hand, and began to rub my hand. It wasn't the movie

Me Tears

type hand holding. She was in the love making holding on to me stage.

"What are you doing?"

"'What?" She replied.

"We are at the movies."

"I bet you that you can't make it home without giving me some." She stated.

Then, the drool came back, and the speech was non-existent, as she pulled my hand to her thigh and let it rest right below the hemline. Yeah, 'G' is for Goodgoogaleemook. Oh, I say it different each time. But, my baby knows just what to do.

..

The AntiVote

Me Tears

Urbn: Opening

From the beginning this is not for those with fragile intellect. Those that think only in the box. Moreover, this book is written and edited by the author. Being from the inner city and a fan of Hip Hop and being just as well in Education as most who are educated. This book is written in the scheme of "Street" rather than the formal 'Standards" of literature. Although the book could have been written with a formal style of writing, my generation is what it is and I support it.

In this view we will look at voting from one who does not vote. The other issue is whether or not we truly have a right to vote. Most important

Me Tears

is the notion that we have a right, a duty, and an obligation not to vote

    The Anti Vote is almost here. In the beginning of this nations birth it was on the outside looking in on it's opportunity. The vote realizes this, and relented on a few occasions. One of those occasions being the civil rights issue. The vote is the physical, or can be said to be the manifestation of the thought of it's national leader at the time vetted by the vote. That's the purpose of election. It vets the candidates to make sure that people don't have a choice. It ensures the status quo. That's why Dr. King was assassinated. His voice came from without the electoral process, like Hip Hop.

    The Anti Vote comes forth into

Me Tears

our lives just as the odor from under our arm pits. If you vote there's the Anti vote. If you wash and put on deodorant, eventually the antiperspirant wears down like the vote. Once you die, there's no need for the deodorant. The vote doesn't win. But, neither does the Anti-Vote. What does happen is change.

The change happened a few times in history. The best example of the Anti vote was the demise of the Roman Empire. The end didn't take place over night per se. The barbarians didn't all of a sudden capture and destroy Rome. They worked the edges. They in some parts became part of the empire, lying dormant for a certain time in space.. It is similar to the actions of the today 'terrorist'.

Me Tears

Eventually they made it to the center. The end came about through a fragile frame and an unstable infrastructure. By infrastructure, reference is being made in terms of morality, and not roads and buildings and public works. The infrastructure here deals with social issues. Although we don't view it as being the same. The same principles apply in war. America has so many views and acceptable ways of doing things that there aren't any right ways versus wrong ways. This is the weakness of America and the Strength of the Middle East. They agree on basic principles. While the United States is divided on the same principles.

    The laws of probability still exists in matter of national security. There

Me Tears

are no 100% certainties in everyday events. So yes, even when the towers fell, not everyone in this land said: "Oh what a shame." This government knows this now and has always known that certain entities within this country is waiting to pounce on the opportunity to end this democracy as we know it. The entity isn't always abroad. Don't think slip of the tongue. How does Dick Chaney know that if the republicans lose the election that there will be another definite terrorist attack?

    Unpatriotic notions brought about the patriot act. What America is viewing is a reflection of America. The picture is not one of an image resembling utopia. The picture is that of destruction, the end. This country is merely a bit of Rome that got away. The part that didn't die. Rome never died , it transformed. Remember this. That which is pure and holy doesn't change. It is the same today, yesterday and tomorrow. Therefore, the Anti-vote didn't die. That same force that sought the end of Rome then, seeks the end to Rome now. The same establishments of the days of ....

Me Tears

Awtuhm Duv 'The Family, The Reunion"—Book II

He was only five years old.
"No son, Regina and Maria had daddy two babies", I answered. "I thought mommy was suppose to have your babies, why you didn't let mommy have more babies daddy?", he continued. The wives began to enjoy this more than they needed to as they wanted an answer as well.
"Shut up" my oldest said.
"Son, you know me and your mommy don't live togther anymore."
"Mommy said you got two bitches", he blurted.
"Daddy got two wives, see" , as I pointed to my wives.
"Which one?" He asked.
"Both", I said.
"Hey, you can't have two wives daddy.", he said.
"Yeah baby, I do," , I assured him as he covered his eyes.
"Daddy can do what he wants, he's the Great Daddini", my oldest daughter added.
"Mommy said you are a whore daddy,", my youngest daughter said, as everyone began to laugh.
"They love me kids and that's the important thing", I tried to end the conversation.
"Mommy still loves you. So, you have three wives." My younger daughter said, as my younger son agreed.

Me Tears

"Both of you cut it out.", my oldest son said.

"Look, one, two, and three, you don't know what you talking about." my daughter said. Then the devil woke. "Let's get it right.", their mother stated as she walked up from behind.

"Hi", she generically spoke. As she commanded the children to follow her to her table. They all gave me kisses and followed their orders hesitantly.

"Why you got a black wife, and a white wife daddy?". My son blurted while he backed away. "Your father is confused.", his mother responded, as she pulled him away and they departed to their table.

"You have some fine babies boy", My mother said.
"Thanks ma", as I gave her a hug. "What's up dad?"

"Hey son, How thangs?", He asked
"No problems," I pushed out, tilting my forehead towards him.

"That's good, you gotta enjoy the peaceful times. That's what a man has to do, bad times are all of ours anyway", he added.
"Ain't that the truth", my mother agreed as she kissed the babies.

"You got two beautiful wives, you is a lucky man."
"Thanks dad", I confirmed, while ma' became less reluctant to agree. Both Regina and Maria smiled and thanked him as well.
"Hey y'all, I'm gonna see you all a bit later, I gotta introduce the wives to the rest of the

Me Tears

peeps."
It was sort of strange in a sense, they both said the same "okay son, sure nice to see y'all made it" at the same time.

"You seen my babies mother before, let's go and introduce you two", I said. Both wives had a smile on their faces as they turned to each other, and adjusted the babies, like women usually adjust their bra. Something about a women having to adjust something before a confrontation. This was not a good thing, but it had to be done. It was a long walk, a reluctant walk, but we arrived to my babies table. My oldest brother's wife was there of course, along with my second oldest sister. Now when it comes to news, these three are the news channel.

"This is my ex-wife Phyllis, and my sister Jean, you all met my brother's wife." I finished.
"Hi", both wives said. My attention was on my oldest daughter, her smile was comforting to me. My oldest son
was sitting in disbelief. He never thought he would see this day, or a day like this. I am sure it was a departure from what he was use to experiencing. Though out my relationship with his mother, I would defer to her. It was probably strange for him to see me reverence other women the way I reverenced his mother. It was strange for me too.

"Hi", all the children returned a hi, while Liza, my oldest just wanted to hold the babies. I could tell, she didn't have to ask. "Give me

Me Tears

Elijah honey", as I reached towards Maria. Me and my daughter had this non verbal type thing going on, even since her birth. I turned my back and as she was sitting closest to my position, I bent down and she immediately reached to hold my baby. My youngest daughter, charged over from across the table. She had a 'if she can, I can mentality'. No one said anything, as their mother folded her arms. My son Andre, he had this look of 'oh shit', on his face, as he tried to ignore the situation.

"Gimme my baby", I said to Liza.

"The Ex-wife, The Underdog, and the Comeback"

    It happened. From the first time I looked into her beautiful brown eyes, I knew she was my Ex-Wife. Not quite knowing what the path was going to be like. I knew for sure that I had to have her.

    Impossible Is the only way to explain this step or mis-step. We know it's not just a fling, but also know that during this time we know it's not going to last long, at least not forever. Forever is what we want when we see love shine through. I had love, but what she had for me was something totally different. She had something unreal, game..

Me Tears

Goons: The Last Days

Before the beginning, that's when. It was all done before the ending. Walking into the future became the difficult part. The day had finally presented itself. The day, the last day.

It was the last sun to moon day. The last morning to night day. Time continued to past as the people began to hear it. They heard it in the voices. It could be felt. The movement of time. So slow the pace, everything, and everyone had a stench. Tomorrow, the time man feared most was presenting itself.

It was a time of man and woman reaching for the next moment and not wanting it. But, that was all that they had. It couldn't be called faith, hope was fleeing. They wanted it to leave, and the other times to return. They didn't want for anything except the morrow without the present within it. However, tomorrow was not for the easing of pain. Tomorrow was for other things contained within it.

In that day, the crow didn't fly as they were stricken. Everything became food for them. They would began to walk the earth as men, and even more bold. For, it was their time. There wasn't any time for man to be with women and women with man. That time had past along with the rapes and suffering of the days gone by. Even those times were better than the present. The good days of predictability had been lost. 'They' were coming..

Me Tears

Me Tears